PRAISE FOR NICCOLÒ AMMANITI AND *I'M NOT SCARED*
WINNER OF THE PRESTIGIOUS VIAREGGIO-REPACI PRIZE

'Against the scorched backdrop of the Italian countryside,
an adult tragedy unfolds from the uncomprehending
perspective of a child.'
La Repubblica

'A tense, breathless book, written with self-confidence
and vitality.'
La Stampa

'Readable in one breath…moving, impressive, amazing. It
reminds you of Italo Calvino, but a Calvino warmed by a
humanity that is not afraid to roll around in the mud.'
Panorama

'Ammaniti, one of the most admired figures on the Italian
fiction scene…uses short sentences like the cracks of a whip
and sharp paragraphs to make our hearts race and carry us
to the edge of the abyss.'
ABC, Spain

'Confirms his extraordinary narrative talent, over which
he superimposes an atmosphere of horror and marvel.'
Le Monde

NICCOLÒ AMMANITI was born in Rome in 1966. He studied biology at university but left before completing his degree. For a time he bred fish and sold them to pet shops—he had twelve aquariums in his room. His failure at studies (and in fish-breeding) were among the themes of his first novel *Branchie*, which was later made into a film. His other books include *Fango*, a collection of stories in various styles (noir, horror, comedy) about the city of Rome, and the novel *Ti prendo e ti porto via*. In 2001 he went to the USA to write *Gone Bad*—a digitally animated splatter comedy about a group of zombies in a Nevada village. Niccolò Ammaniti lives in Italy.

I'm Not Scared was first published in Italy in 2001 where it became a major bestseller. It has been translated into twenty languages and a film based on the novel, directed by Gabriele Salvatores, is now in production.

JONATHAN HUNT has worked as a literary translator for several years and has taught at universities in Munich, Cambridge and Turin. He holds a research post at Turin University.

I'm Not Scared

Niccolò Ammaniti

translated by Jonathan Hunt

t

TEXT PUBLISHING
MELBOURNE AUSTRALIA

The Text Publishing Company
171 La Trobe Street
Melbourne Victoria 3000 Australia

Io non ho paura first published by Giulio Einaudi Editore 2001
This translation first published by Canongate Books Ltd 2003
This edition published by The Text Publishing Company 2003

Printed and bound by Griffin Press
Typeset in Baskerville MT by J & M Typesetting

National Library of Australia
Cataloguing-in-Publication data:

Ammaniti, Niccolò, 1966- .
I'm not scared.
1st Australian ed.
ISBN 1 877008 46 X.
1. Children's secrets - Fiction. 2. Italy - Fiction. I.
Hunt, Jonathan. II. Title

853.914

This book is dedicated to my sister Luisa,
who followed me on the Nera
with her little silver star
pinned to her jacket.

'That much he knew. He had fallen into darkness. And at the instant he knew, he ceased to know.'

Jack London

I WAS just about to overtake Salvatore when I heard my sister scream. I turned and saw her disappear, swallowed up by the wheat that covered the hill.

I shouldn't have brought her along. Mama would be furious with me.

I stopped. I was sweaty. I got my breath back and called to her, 'Maria? Maria?'

A plaintive little voice answered me. 'Michele.'

'Have you hurt yourself?'

'Yes, come here.'

'Where've you hurt yourself?'

'On the leg.'

She was faking, she was tired. I'm going on, I said to myself. But what if she really was hurt?

Where were the others?

I saw their tracks in the wheat. They were rising slowly, in parallel lines, like the fingers of a hand, towards the top of the hill, leaving a wake of trampled stalks behind them.

The wheat was high that year. In late spring it had rained a lot, and by mid-June the stalks were higher and more luxuriant than ever. They grew densely packed, heavy-eared, ready to be harvested.

Everything was covered in wheat. The low hills rolled away like the waves of a golden ocean. As far as the horizon nothing but wheat, sky, crickets, sun and heat.

I had no idea how hot it was, degrees centigrade don't mean much to a nine-year-old, but I knew it wasn't normal.

That damned summer of 1978 has gone down in history as one of the hottest of the century. The heat got into the stones, crumbled the earth, scorched the plants and killed the livestock, made the houses sweltering. When you picked the tomatoes in the vegetable garden they had no juice and the zucchini were small and hard. The sun took away your breath, your strength, your desire to play, everything. And it was just as unbearable at night.

At Acqua Traverse the grown-ups didn't leave the houses till six in the evening. They shut themselves up indoors with the blinds drawn. Only we chidren ventured out into the fiery deserted countryside.

My sister Maria was five and followed me as stubbornly as a little mongrel rescued from a dog pound.

'I want to do what you do,' she always said. Mama backed her up.

'Are you or are you not her big brother?' And there was nothing for it, I had to take her along.

No one had stopped to help her.

After all, it was a race.

'Straight up the hill. No curves. No following each other. No stopping. Last one there pays a forfeit,' Skull had decided and he had conceded to me: 'All right, your sister's not in the race. She's too small.'

'I'm not too small!' Maria had protested. 'I want to race too!' And then she had fallen down.

Pity, I was lying third.

First was Antonio. As usual.

Antonio Natale, known as Skull. Why we called him Skull I can't remember. Maybe because once he had stuck a skull on his arm, one of those transfers you bought at the tobacconist's and fixed on with water. Skull was the oldest in the gang. Twelve years old. And he was the chief. He liked giving orders and if you didn't obey he turned nasty. He was no Einstein, but he was big, strong and brave. And he was going up that hill like a goddam bulldozer.

Second was Salvatore.

Salvatore Scardaccione was nine, the same age as me. We were classmates. He was my best friend. Salvatore was taller than me. He was a loner. Sometimes he came with us but often he kept to himself. He was brighter than Skull, and could easily have deposed him, but he wasn't interested in becoming chief. His father, the Avvocato Emilio Scardaccione, was a big shot in Rome. And had a lot of money stashed away in Switzerland. That's what they said, anyway.

Then there was me, Michele. Michele Amitrano. And I was third that time, yet again. I had been going well, but now, thanks to my sister, I was at a standstill.

I was debating whether to turn back or leave her there, when I found myself in fourth place. On the other side of the ridge that duffer Remo Marzano had overtaken me.

And if I didn't start climbing again straight away Barbara Mura would overtake me too.

That would be awful. Overtaken by a girl. And a fat one too.

Barbara Mura was scrambling up on all fours like a demented sow. All sweaty and covered in earth.

'Hey, aren't you going back for your little sister? Didn't you hear her? She's hurt herself, poor little thing,' she grunted happily. For once it wasn't going to be her who paid the forfeit.

'I'm going, I'm going…And I'll beat you too.' I couldn't admit defeat to her just like that.

I turned and started back down, waving my arms and whooping like a Sioux. My leather sandals slipped on the wheat. I fell down on my backside a couple of times.

I couldn't see her. 'Maria! Maria! Where are you?'

'Michele…'

There she was. Small and unhappy. Sitting on a ring of broken stalks. Rubbing her ankle with one hand and holding her glasses in the other. Her hair was stuck to her forehead and her eyes were moist. When she saw me she twisted her mouth and swelled up like a turkey.

'Michele?'

'Maria, you've made me lose the race! I told you not to come, damn you.' I sat down. 'What have you done?'

'I tripped up. I hurt my foot and…' She threw her mouth wide open, screwed up her eyes, shook her head and exploded into a wail. 'My glasses! My glasses are broken!'

I could have thumped her. It was the third time she had broken her glasses since school had finished. And every time, who did mama blame?

'You've got to look after your sister, you're her big brother.'

'Mama, I…'

'I don't want to hear any of your excuses. It hasn't sunk into your head yet, but I don't find money in the vegetable garden. The next time you break those glasses I'll give you such a hiding…'

They had snapped in the middle, where they had already been stuck together once before. They were a write-off.

Meanwhile my sister kept on crying.

'Mama…She'll be cross…What are we going to do?'

'What else can we do? Stick them together with Scotch tape. Up you get, come on.'

'They look horrible with Scotch tape. Really horrible. I don't like them.'

I put the glasses in my pocket. Without them my sister couldn't see a thing, she had a squint and the doctor had said she would have to have an operation before she grew up. 'Never mind. Up you get.'

She stopped crying and started sniffing. 'My foot hurts.'

'Where?' I kept thinking of the others, they must have reached the top of the hill ages ago. I was last. I only hoped Skull wouldn't make me do too tough a forfeit. Once when I had lost a bike race he had made me run through nettles.

'Where does it hurt?'

'Here.' She showed me her ankle.

'You've twisted it. It's nothing. It'll soon stop hurting.'

I unlaced her trainer and took it off very carefully. As a doctor would have done. 'Is that better?'

'A bit. Shall we go home? I'm terribly thirsty. And mama…'

She was right. We had come too far. And we had been out too long. It was way past lunchtime and mama would be on the lookout at the window.

I wasn't looking forward to our return home.

But who would have thought it a few hours earlier.

That morning we had gone off on our bikes.

Usually we went for short rides, round the houses. We cycled as far as the edges of the fields, the dried-up stream, and raced each other back.

My bike was an old boneshaker, with a patched-up saddle, and so high I had to lean right over to touch the ground.

Everyone called it 'the Crock'. Salvatore said it was the bike the Alpine troops had used in the war. But I liked it, it was my father's.

If we didn't go cycling we stayed in the street playing football, steal-the-flag, or one-two-three-star, or lounged under the shed roof doing nothing.

We could do whatever we liked. No cars ever went by. There were no dangers. And the grown-ups stayed shut up indoors, like toads waiting for the heat to die down.

Time passed slowly. By the end of the summer we were longing for school to start again.

That morning we had been talking about Melichetti's pigs.

We often talked about Melichetti's pigs. Rumour had it old Melichetti trained them to savage hens, and sometimes rabbits and cats he found by the roadside.

Skull spat out a spray of white saliva. 'I've never told you till now. Because I couldn't say. But now I *will* tell you: those pigs ate Melichetti's daughter's dachshund.'

A general chorus arose, 'No, they couldn't have!'

'They did. I swear on the heart of the Madonna. Alive. Completely alive.'

'It's not possible!'

What sort of monsters must they be to eat a pedigree dog?

Skull nodded. 'Melichetti threw it into the pigsty. The dachshund tried to get away, they're crafty animals, but Melichetti's pigs are craftier. Didn't give him a chance. Torn to shreds in two seconds.' Then he added, 'Worse than wild boars.'

Barbara asked him, 'But why did he throw it to them?'

Skull thought for a moment. 'It pissed in the house. And if *you* fall in there, you fat lump, they'll strip all the flesh off you, right down to the bone.'

Maria stood up. 'Is Melichetti crazy?'

Skull spat on the ground again. 'Crazier than his pigs.'

We were silent for a few moments imagining Melichetti's daughter with such a wicked father. None of us knew her name, but she was famous for having a sort of iron brace round one leg.

'We could go and see them!' I suggested suddenly.

'An expedition!' said Barbara.

'It's a long way away, Melichetti's farm. It'd take ages,' Salvatore grumbled.

'No, it isn't, it's not far at all, let's go…' Skull got on his bike. He never missed a chance to put Salvatore down.

I had an idea. 'Why don't we take a hen from Remo's chicken run, so when we get there we can throw it into the pigsty and see how they tear it apart?'

'Brilliant!' Skull approved.

'But papa will kill me if we take one of his hens,' Remo wailed.

It was no use, the idea was a really good one.

We went into the chicken run, chose the thinnest, scrawniest hen and stuck it in a bag.

And off we went, all six of us and the hen, to see those famous pigs of Melichetti's, and we pedalled along between the wheatfields, and as we pedalled the sun rose and roasted everything.

Salvatore was right, Melichetti's farm was a long way away. By the time we got there we were parched and our heads were boiling.

Melichetti was sitting, with sunglasses on, in a rusty old rocking chair under a crooked beach umbrella.

The house was falling to pieces and the roof had been roughly patched up with tin and tar. In the farmyard there was a heap of rubbish: wheels, a rusty Bianchina, some bottomless chairs, a table with one leg missing. On an ivy-covered wooden post hung some cows' skulls, worn by the rain and sun. And a smaller skull with no horns. Goodness knows what animal that came from.

A great big dog, all skin and bone, barked on a chain.

Behind the house were some corrugated iron huts and the pigsties, on the edge of a gravina.

Gravinas are small canyons, long crevasses dug by the

water in the rock. White spires, rocks and pointed crags protrude from the red earth. Inside, twisted olive trees, arbutuses and holly often grow, and there are caves where the shepherds put their sheep.

Melichetti looked like a mummy. His wrinkled skin hung off him, and he was hairless, except for a white tuft in the middle of his chest. Round his neck he had an orthopaedic collar fastened with green elastic bands, and he was wearing black shorts and brown plastic flipflops.

He had seen us arrive on our bikes, but he didn't move. We must have seemed like a mirage to him. Nobody ever passed by on that road, except the occasional truck carrying hay.

There was a smell of piss. And millions of horseflies. They didn't bother Melichetti. They settled on his head and round his eyes, like they do on cows. Only if they got on his lips did he react, puffing them away.

Skull stepped forward. 'Signore, we're thirsty. Have you got any water?'

I was worried, because a man like Melichetti was liable to shoot you, throw you to the pigs, or give you poisoned water to drink. Papa had told me about a guy in America who had a pond where he kept crocodiles, and if you stopped to ask him the way he would ask you in, knock you on the head and feed you to the crocodiles. And when the police had come, rather than go to prison he had let his pets tear him to pieces. Melichetti could easily be that sort of guy.

The old man raised his sunglasses. 'What are you doing here, kids? Aren't you a bit far from home?'

'Signor Melichetti, is it true you fed your dachshund to

the pigs?' Barbara piped up.

I could have died. Skull turned and gave her a glare of hatred. Salvatore kicked her in the shin.

Melichetti burst out laughing, had a fit of coughing and nearly choked. When he had recovered he said, 'Who tells you these daft stories, little girl?'

Barbara pointed at Skull. 'He does!'

Skull blushed, hung his head and looked at his shoes.

I knew why Barbara had said it.

A few days earlier we had had a stone-throwing competition and Barbara had lost. As a forfeit Skull had ordered her to unbutton her shirt and show us her breasts. Barbara was eleven. She had a small bosom, just flea-bites, nothing to what she would have in a couple of years' time. She had refused. 'If you don't, you can forget about coming with us any more,' Skull had threatened her. I had felt bad about it, the forfeit wasn't fair. I didn't like Barbara, as soon as she got the chance she would try to pull a fast one on you, but showing her tits, no, that seemed too much.

Skull had decided. 'Either show us your tits or get lost.'

And Barbara, without a word, had gone ahead and unbuttoned her shirt.

I couldn't help looking at them. They were the first tits I had seen in my life, except for mama's. Maybe once, when she had come to stay with us, I had seen my cousin Evelina's, she was ten years older than me. Anyway, I had already formed an idea of the sort of tits I liked, and Barbara's I didn't like at all. They looked like scamorzas, folds of skin, not much different from the rolls of fat on her stomach.

Barbara had been brooding on that episode and now she meant to get even with Skull.

10

'So you go around telling people I fed my dachshund to the pigs.' Melichetti scratched his chest. 'Augustus, that dog was called. Like the Roman emperor. Thirteen he was, when he died. Got a chicken bone stuck in his throat. Had a Christian funeral, proper grave and all.' He pointed his finger at Skull. 'I bet you're the oldest, aren't you, little boy?'

Skull didn't reply.

'You must never tell lies. And you mustn't blacken other people's names. You must tell the truth, especially to those who are younger than you. The truth, always. Before men, before the Lord God, and before yourself.' He sounded like a priest delivering a sermon.

'Didn't he even pee in the house?' Barbara persisted.

Melichetti tried to shake his head, but the collar prevented him. 'He was a well-behaved dog. Great mouser. God rest his soul.' He pointed towards the drinking trough. 'If you're thirsty there's water over there. The best in the whole area. And that's no lie.'

We drank till we were bursting. It was cool and sweet. Then we started spraying each other, and sticking our heads under the spout.

Skull said Melichetti was a piece of shit. And he knew for a fact the old fool had fed the dachshund to the pigs.

He scowled at Barbara and said, 'I'll get you for this.' He walked off muttering and sat down by himself on the other side of the road.

Salvatore, Remo and I set about catching tadpoles. My sister and Barbara perched on the edge of the trough and dipped their feet in the water.

After a few minutes Skull came back, all excited.

'Look! Look! Look at the size of it!'

We turned round. 'What?'

'That.'

It was a hill.

It looked like a panettone. A huge panettone that some giant had placed on the plain. It rose in front of us a couple of kilometres away. Golden and immense. The wheat covered it like a fur coat. There wasn't a tree, a crag, a blemish, to spoil its outline. The sky, around it, was liquid and dirty. The other hills, behind, were like dwarves compared to that huge dome.

Goodness knows how none of us had noticed it till that moment. We had seen it, but without really seeing it. Maybe because it blended in with the landscape. Maybe because we had all had our eyes glued to the road looking out for Melichetti's farm.

'Let's climb it.' Skull pointed at it. 'Let's climb that mountain.'

I said, 'I wonder what's up on top.'

It must be an incredible place, maybe some strange animal lived there. None of us had ever been up so high.

Salvatore screened his eyes with his hand and scanned the top. 'I bet you can see the sea from up there. Yes, we must climb it.'

We gazed at it in silence.

Now that *was* an adventure, damn Melichetti's pigs.

'And we'll put our flag on the summit. So if anyone climbs up there, they'll know we got there first,' I said.

'What flag? We haven't got a flag,' said Salvatore.

'We'll use the hen.'

Skull grabbed the bag with the bird in it and whirled it round in the air. 'Right! We'll wring its neck, then we'll put

12

a stick up its arse and fix it in the ground. The skeleton will be left there. I'll carry it up.'

An impaled hen might be taken as a sign of witchcraft.

But Skull pulled out his ace. 'Straight up the hill. No curves. No following each other. No stopping. Last one there pays a forfeit.'

We were speechless.

A race! Why?

It was obvious. To get his own back on Barbara. She would come last and would have to pay.

I thought of my sister. I said she was too small to race and it wasn't fair, she would lose.

Barbara gestured no with her finger. She had twigged the little surprise Skull was planning for her.

'So what? A race is a race. She came with us. Otherwise she has to wait for us down here.'

That wasn't on. I couldn't leave Maria. The crocodile story kept going round and round in my head. Melichetti had been kind, but it didn't do to be too trusting. If he killed her, what was I going to tell mama?

'If my sister stays behind, I stay behind.'

Maria piped up. 'I'm not small! I want to race.'

'You shut up!'

Skull settled it. She could come, but she wouldn't be in the race.

We dumped our bikes behind the drinking trough and set off.

That was why I was up on that hill.

I put Maria's trainer back on.

'Can you walk?'

'No. It hurts too much.'

'Wait a minute.' I blew twice on her leg. Then I dug my hands in the hot earth. I picked up a small amount, spat on it and spread it on her ankle. 'That'll make it better.' I knew it wouldn't work. Earth was good for bee stings and nettles, not twisted ankles, but Maria might fall for it. 'Is that better?'

She wiped her nose with her arm. 'A bit.'

'Can you walk?'

'Yes.'

I took her hand. 'Let's get going then. Come on, we're last.'

We set off towards the top. Every five minutes Maria had to sit down to rest her leg. Luckily a bit of wind had got up, which improved things. It rustled in the wheat, making a noise that sounded like breathing. Once I thought I saw an animal pass by us. Black, swift, silent. A wolf? There weren't any wolves in our area. Maybe a fox or a dog.

The climb was steep and never-ending. All I had in front of my eyes was wheat, but when I started to see a slice of sky I understood that it wasn't far now, the top was there, and without even realising it we were standing on the summit.

There was absolutely nothing special about it. It was covered with wheat like all the rest. Under our feet was the same red, baked earth. Above our heads the same blazing sun.

I looked at the horizon. A milky haze veiled things. You couldn't see the sea. But you could see the other, lower hills, and Melichetti's farm with its pigsties and the gravina, and you could see the white road cutting across the fields, that long road we had cycled down to get there. And, tiny in the distance, you could see the hamlet where we lived. Acqua Traverse. Four little houses and an old country villa lost in the wheat. Lucignano, the neighbouring village, was hidden by the mist.

My sister said, 'I want to look too. Let me look.'

I lifted her on my shoulders, though I was so tired I could hardly stand. God knows what she saw without her glasses.

'Where are the others?'

Where they had passed, the regularity of the ears of wheat had gone, many stalks were bent in half and some were broken. We followed the tracks that led towards the other side of the hill.

Maria squeezed my hand and dug her nails into my skin. 'Ugh! How horrible!'

I turned.

They had done it. They had impaled the hen. It was there on top of a stick. Legs dangling, wings outspread. As if, before yielding up its soul to the Creator, it had abandoned itself to its executioners. Its head hung on one side like a ghastly blood-soaked pendant. Heavy red drops dripped from the parted beak. And the end of the stick emerged from the breast. A swarm of metallised flies buzzed around it and clustered on the eyes, on the blood.

A shiver ran up my back.

We went on and after crossing the backbone of the hill we began to descend.

Where on earth had the others got to? Why had they gone down that way?

We walked another twenty metres and found out.

The hill wasn't round. Behind, it lost its faultless perfection. It lengthened out into a kind of hump that wound its way gently down till it joined the plain. In the middle there was a narrow, enclosed valley, invisible except from up there or from an aeroplane.

It would be easy to make a clay model of that hill. Just form a ball. Cut it in half. Place one half on the table. Make the other into a sausage, a sort of fat worm, and stick it on behind, leaving a little hollow in the middle.

The strange thing was that inside that concealed hollow some trees had grown. Sheltered from the wind and sun there was a little oak wood. And an abandoned house, with a ramshackle roof, brown tiles and dark beams, stood out among the green foliage.

We went down the path and entered the valley.

It was the last thing I would have expected. Trees. Shade. Cool.

You couldn't hear the crickets any more, only the twittering of birds. There were purple cyclamen. And carpets of green ivy. And a pleasant smell. It made you feel like finding yourself a cosy little spot by a tree trunk and having a nap.

Salvatore appeared suddenly, like a ghost. 'What do you think of this place then? Isn't it great?'

'Fantastic!' I replied, looking around. Maybe there was a stream to drink from.

'What took you so long? I thought you'd gone back down.'

'No, my sister's foot was hurting, so…I'm thirsty. I need a drink.'

Salvatore took a bottle out of his rucksack. 'There's not much left.'

Maria and I went halves. It was barely enough to wet our lips.

'Who won the race?' I was worried about the forfeit. I was worn out. I hoped Skull, for once, might let me off or postpone it to another day.

'Skull.'

'Where did you come?'

'Second. Remo was third.'

'What about Barbara?'

'Last.'

'Who's got to do the forfeit?'

'Skull says Barbara's got to do it. But Barbara says you've got to do it because you came last.'

'So?'

'I don't know, I went off for a walk. I'm fed up with all these forfeits.'

We started walking towards the farmhouse.

It was a really tumbledown place. It stood in the middle of a clearing covered by the branches of the oaks. Deep cracks ran up from the foundations to the roof. All that was left of the windowpanes was a few shards. A fig tree, all tangled, had overgrown the stairway that led up to the balcony. The roots had dismantled the stone steps and brought down the parapet. At the top there was still an old light-blue door, rotten to the core and peeled by the sun. In the middle of the building a big arch opened on to a room with a vaulted ceiling. A cowshed. Rusty props and

17

wooden poles supported the upper floor, which in many places had fallen through. The ground was littered with dried-up dung, ash, and heaps of broken tiles and brick. The walls had lost most of their plaster and showed the dry stonework behind.

Skull was sitting on a water tank. He was throwing stones at a rusty drum and watching us. 'You made it.' And he added pointedly, 'This place is mine.'

'What do you mean it's yours?'

'I saw it first. Finders keepers.'

I was pushed forward and nearly fell flat on my face. I turned round.

Barbara, with red face, dirty T-shirt and ruffled hair, came at me, spoiling for a punch-up. 'You've got to do it. You came last. You lost!'

I put up my fists. 'I went back. Otherwise I'd have been third. You know that.'

'So what? You lost!'

'Who's got to do the forfeit?' I asked Skull. 'Me or her?'

He took his time before answering, then pointed at Barbara.

'See? See?' I loved Skull.

Barbara started kicking at the dust. 'It's not fair! It's not fair! Always me! Why's it always me?'

I didn't know why. But even then I knew that someone always gets all the bad luck. During those days it was Barbara Mura, the fat girl, she was the lamb that took away the sins.

I was sorry, but I was glad I wasn't in her shoes.

Barbara stomped round among us like a rhinoceros.

'Let's vote on it, then! He can't decide everything.'

Even after twenty-two years I still don't understand how she put up with us. It must have been the fear of being left on her own.

'All right. Let's vote on it,' Skull conceded. 'I say it's you.'

'So do I,' I said.

'So do I,' parroted Maria.

We looked at Salvatore. No one could abstain when there was a vote. That was the rule.

'So do I,' said Salvatore, almost in a whisper.

'See? Five one. You've lost. You do it,' Skull concluded.

Barbara tightened her lips and her fists, I saw her swallow a lump the size of a tennis ball. She dropped her head, but she didn't cry.

I respected her.

'What…do I have to do?' she stammered.

Skull rubbed his throat. His sadistic mind got to work.

He wavered for a moment. 'You've got to…show it to us…You've got to show it to all of us.'

Barbara swayed. 'What have I got to show to you?'

'Last time you showed us your tits.' And turning to us, 'This time you're going to show us your slit. Your hairy slit. You pull down your knickers and you show it to us.' He burst into raucous laughter, expecting that we would do the same, but we didn't. We froze, as if a wind from the North Pole had suddenly blown into the valley.

The forfeit was too harsh. None of us wanted to see Barbara's slit. It was a punishment for us as well. My stomach tightened. I wished I was far away. There was something dirty, something…I don't know. Something nasty, that's all. And I didn't like my sister being there.

'Forget it,' said Barbara shaking her head. 'I don't

care if you hit me.'

Skull got up and strolled towards her with his hands in his pockets. Between his teeth he had an ear of wheat.

He stood in front of her. He craned his neck. He wasn't all that much taller than Barbara. Or stronger. I wasn't so sure he would beat her all that easily if they had a fight. If Barbara threw him on the ground and jumped on him she might even smother him.

'You lost. Now pull down your trousers. That'll teach you to fuck me around.'

'No!'

Skull slapped her across the face.

Barbara opened her mouth like a trout and rubbed her cheek. She still wasn't crying. She turned towards us.

'Haven't you lot got anything to say?' she whimpered. 'You're just as bad as him!'

We remained silent.

'All right then. But you'll never see me again. I swear it on my mother's head.'

'What's the matter, are you crying?' Skull was revelling in it.

'No, I'm not,' she managed to say, suppressing her sobs.

She was wearing green cotton trousers with brown patches on the knees, the sort you could buy at the flea market. They were too tight for her and her flab bulged out over the belt. She opened the buckle and started to undo her buttons.

I caught a glimpse of white knickers with little yellow flowers. 'Wait! I came last,' I heard my voice saying.

Everyone turned.

'Yes,' I gulped. 'I want to do it.'

'What?' Remo asked me.

'The forfeit.'

'No. She's got to,' Skull snapped at me. 'It's nothing to do with you. Shut up.'

'Yes it is. I came last. I've got to do it.'

'No. I decide.' Skull came towards me.

My legs were shaking, but I hoped nobody would notice. 'Let's have another vote.'

Salvatore got between me and Skull. 'Second votes are allowed.'

We had certain rules and one of them was that second votes were allowed.

I raised my hand. 'I do the forfeit.'

Salvatore put up his hand. 'Michele does it.'

Barbara fastened her belt and sobbed. 'He does it. It's only fair.'

Skull was caught by surprise, he stared at Remo with his mad eyes. 'What do you say?'

Remo sighed. 'Barbara does it.'

'What shall I do?' asked Maria.

I nodded to her.

'My brother does it.'

'Four two,' Salvatore said. 'Michele's won. He does it.'

Getting up to the first floor of the house wasn't easy.

The stairway no longer existed. The steps had been reduced to a heap of stone blocks. I was working my way up by holding onto the branches of the fig tree. The brambles scratched my arms and legs. One thorn had grazed my right cheek.

Walking up the parapet was out of the question. If it had given way I would have fallen into a mass of nettles and briars.

This was the forfeit I had landed myself with by playing the hero.

'You've got to climb up to the first floor. Get in. Go right across the house, jump out of the end window onto the tree and climb down.'

I had been afraid Skull would make me show my dick or poke a stick up my arse, but instead he had chosen to make me do something dangerous, where the worst that could happen was that I might get hurt.

That was something, anyway.

I gritted my teeth and went on without complaining. The others were sitting under an oak enjoying the spectacle of Michele Amitrano risking his neck.

Every now and then a bit of advice arrived: 'Go that way.' 'You've got to keep straight on, it's full of brambles round there.' 'Eat a blackberry, it'll do you good.'

I took no notice.

I was up on the balcony. There was a narrow space between the brambles and the wall. I squeezed through and got to the doorway. It was fastened with a chain but the padlock was eaten away by rust and had come open. I pushed one flap and with a metallic groan the doors gave way.

A great fluttering of wings. Feathers. A flock of pigeons took off and flew out through a hole in the roof.

'What's it like? What's it like inside?' I heard Skull ask.

I didn't bother to reply. I went in, watching where I put my feet.

I was in a big room. A lot of roof tiles had fallen off and a beam was hanging down in the middle. In one corner there was a fireplace with a pyramid-shaped hood that was blackened by smoke. In another corner some furniture was piled up. An overturned rusty cooker. Bottles. Bits of crockery. Roof tiles. A broken bedspring. Everything was covered in pigeon shit. And there was a strong smell, an acrid stench that got right into your nose and throat. A forest of wild plants and weeds had sprung up through the tiled floor. At the other end of the room was a closed red door which no doubt led to the other rooms of the house.

That was the way I had to go.

I put one foot down, under my soles the beams creaked and the floor lurched. At the time I weighed about thirty-five kilos. About as much as a tank of water. I wondered if a tank of water, placed in the middle of that room, would bring the floor down. I didn't think I'd try it.

To reach the next door it was more prudent to keep right against the walls. Holding my breath, on tiptoe like a ballerina, I followed the perimeter of the room. If the floor gave way I would fall into the cowshed, after a drop of at least four metres. I could easily break a few bones.

But it didn't happen.

In the next room, which was about the same size as the kitchen, the floor had completely gone. At the sides it had collapsed and only a sort of bridge now connected my door to the one on the other side. Of the six beams that had supported the floor only the two middle ones were sound. The others were worm-eaten stumps.

I couldn't follow the walls. I would have to cross that bridge. The beams supporting it couldn't be in a much better condition than the others.

I was paralysed in the doorway. I couldn't turn back. They would taunt me with it for ever more. What if I jumped down? Suddenly those four metres that separated me from the cowshed didn't seem so far. I could tell the others it was impossible to reach the window.

The brain plays nasty tricks sometimes.

About ten years later I happened to go skiing on the Gran Sasso. It was the wrong day—it was snowing, bitterly cold, with an icy wind that froze your ears and a thick mist. I had only ever been skiing once before. I was really excited and I didn't care if everybody said it was dangerous, I wanted to ski. I got on the ski lift, muffled up like an eskimo, and headed for the slopes.

The wind was so strong that the lift motor switched off automatically, and only started again when the gusts died down. It would move ten metres, then stop for a quarter of an hour, then another forty metres and twenty minutes without moving. And so on, *ad infinitum*. Maddening. As far as I could make out the rest of the ski lift was empty. Gradually I started to lose all feeling in my toes, my ears, my fingers. I tried to brush the snow off me, but it was a wasted effort, it fell silently, lightly and incessantly.

After a while I started to get drowsy and think more slowly. I pulled myself together and told myself that if I fell asleep I would die. I shouted for help. Only the wind replied. I looked down. I was directly over a ski run. Suspended about ten metres above the snow. I thought back to the story of that airman who during the war had jumped out of his burning aircraft and his parachute hadn't opened but he hadn't been killed, he had been saved by the soft snow. Ten metres weren't all that far. If I jumped well, if I didn't stiffen up, I wouldn't get hurt; the parachutist hadn't got hurt. Part of my brain repeated to me obsessively, 'Jump! Jump! Jump!' I lifted the safety bar. And I started to rock backwards and forwards. Luckily at that moment the ski lift moved and I regained my senses. I lowered the bar. It was incredibly high, at the very least I would have broken both my legs.

In that house I had the same feeling. I wanted to jump down. Then I remembered reading in one of Salvatore's books that lizards can climb up walls because they have perfect weight distribution. They spread their weight over their legs, stomach and tail, whereas human beings put all theirs on their feet and that's why they sink into quicksand.

Yes, that was what I must do.

I knelt down, lay flat and started to crawl along. At every movement I made, bits of masonry and tiles fell down. Light, light as a lizard, I repeated to myself. I felt the beams quiver. It took me a full five minutes but I reached the other side safe and sound.

I pushed the door. It was the last one. At the other end was the window that overlooked the yard. A long branch snaked across to the house. I had made it. Here too the floor had fallen through, but only half of it. The other half had held. I used the old technique, walking flat against the wall. Below I could see another dimly lit room. There were the remains of a fire, some opened cans of tomatoes and empty packets of pasta. Somebody must have been there not long ago.

I reached the window without mishap. I looked down. There was a small yard skirted by a row of brambles and the wood behind it pressing in. On the ground there was a cracked cement trough, a rusty crane jib, piles of masonry covered in ivy, a gas cylinder and a mattress.

The branch I had to get onto was close—less than a metre away. Not close enough, however, to be reachable without jumping. It was thick and twisty like an anaconda. It stretched over more than five metres. It would carry my weight. Once I reached the other end I would find a way to get down.

I stood up on the windowsill, crossed myself, and threw myself arms first, like a gibbon in the Amazon forest. I landed face down on the branch. I tried to grip it, but it was big. I used my legs but there was nothing to get hold of. I started to slip. I tried to claw onto the bark.

Salvation was right in front of me. There was a smaller branch just a few dozen centimetres away.

I steeled myself and with a sudden lunge grabbed it with both hands.

It was dry. It snapped.

I landed on my back. I lay still, with my eyes closed, certain I had broken my neck. I couldn't feel any pain. I lay there, petrified, with the branch in my hands, trying to understand why I wasn't suffering. Maybe I had become a paralytic who, even if you stub out a cigarette on his arm and stick a fork into his thigh, doesn't feel a thing.

I opened my eyes. I gazed at the vast green umbrella of the oak that loomed over me. The glittering of the sun between the leaves. I must try and raise my head. I raised it.

I threw that stupid branch away. I touched the ground with my hands. And I discovered I was on something soft. The mattress.

I had a flashback of myself falling, flying and crashing down without hurting myself. There had been a dull, hollow sound at the exact moment I had landed. I had heard it, I could have sworn it.

I moved my feet and discovered that under the leaves, the twigs and the earth there was a green corrugated sheet, a transparent fibreglass roof. It had been covered up, as if to hide it. And that old mattress had been put on top of it.

It was the corrugated sheet that had saved me. It had bent and absorbed the force of my fall.

So underneath it must be hollow.

It might be a secret hiding place or a tunnel leading to a cave full of gold and precious stones.

I got down on my hands and knees and pushed the sheet forward.

It was heavy, but gradually I managed to shift it a little. A terrible stink of shit was released.

I swayed, put one hand over my mouth and pushed again.

I had fallen on top of a hole.

It was dark. But the further I shifted the fibreglass sheet the lighter it became. The walls were made of earth, dug with a spade. The roots of the oak had been cut.

I managed to move it a bit further. The hole was a couple of metres wide and two, two and a half metres deep.

It was empty.

No, there was something there.

A heap of rolled-up rags?

No...

An animal? A dog? No...

What was it?

It was hairless…

white…

a leg…

A leg!

I jumped backwards and nearly tripped over.

A leg?

I took a deep breath and had a quick look down.

It was a leg.

I felt my ears boil, my head and arms hang heavy.

I was going to pass out.

I sat down, shut my eyes, rested my forehead on one hand, and breathed in. I was tempted to run away, run to the others. But I couldn't. I had to have another look first.

I went forward and peered over.

It was a boy's leg. And sticking out of the rags was an elbow.

At the bottom of that hole there was a boy.

He was lying on one side. His head was hidden between his legs.

He wasn't moving.

He was dead.

I stood looking at him for God knows how long. There was a bucket too. And a little saucepan.

Maybe he was asleep.

I picked up a small stone and threw it at the boy. I hit him on the thigh. He didn't move. He was dead. Dead as a doornail. A shiver bit the back of my head. I picked up another stone and hit him on the neck. I thought he moved. A slight movement of the arm.

'Where are you? Where are you? Where've you got to, you pansy?'

The others! Skull was calling me.

I grabbed the corrugated sheet and pulled it till it covered the hole. Then I spread out the leaves and earth and put the mattress back on top.

'Where are you, Michele?'

I went away, but first I turned round a couple of times to check that everything was in place.

I was pedalling along on the Crock.

The sun behind me was a huge red ball, and when it finally sank into the wheat it disappeared leaving behind it something orange and purple.

They had asked me how I had got on in the house, if it had been dangerous, if I had fallen down, if there were any strange things in there, if jumping onto the tree had been difficult. I had answered in monosyllables.

Finally, bored, we had started back. A path led out of the valley, crossed the ochre fields and reached the road. We had collected our bikes and were pedalling along in silence. Swarms of midges hummed around us.

I looked at Maria, who was following me on her Graziella with its tyres worn by the stones, Skull, out in front, with his squire Remo beside him, Salvatore zigzagging along, Barbara on her oversize Bianchi, and I thought about the boy in the hole.

I wasn't going to say anything to anyone.

'Finders keepers,' Skull had decided.

If that was so, the boy at the bottom of the hole was mine.

If I told them, Skull, as always, would take all the credit

for the discovery. He would tell everyone he had found him because it had been his decision to climb the hill.

Not this time. I had done the forfeit, I had fallen out of the tree and I had found him.

He wasn't Skull's. He wasn't Barbara's either. He wasn't Salvatore's. He was mine. He was my secret discovery.

I didn't know if I had discovered a dead person or a living one. Maybe the arm hadn't moved. I had imagined it. Or maybe they were the contractions of a corpse. Like those of wasps, which keep on walking even if you cut them in two with scissors, or like chickens, which flap their wings even when they've lost their heads. But what was he doing in there?

'What are we going to tell mama?'

I hadn't noticed my sister was riding beside me. 'What?'

'What are we going to tell mama?'

'I don't know.'

'Will you tell her about the glasses?'

'Okay, but you mustn't tell her anything about where we went. If she finds out she'll say you broke them because we went up there.'

'All right.'

'Swear.'

'I swear.' She kissed her forefingers.

Nowadays Acqua Traverse is a district of Lucignano. In the mid-eighties a local building surveyor put up two long rows of houses made of reinforced concrete. Cubes with round windows, light blue railings and iron rods sticking out of the roofs. Then a co-op arrived and a bar-cum-tobacconist's. And an asphalted two-way road that runs straight as an airport runway to Lucignano.

In 1978 Acqua Traverse was so small it was practically non-existent. A country hamlet, they would call it nowadays in a travel magazine.

No one knew why it was called Acqua Traverse, not even old Tronca. There certainly wasn't any water there, except what they brought in a tanker once a fortnight.

There was Salvatore's villa, which we called the Palazzo. A big house built in the nineteenth century, long and grey with a big stone porch and an inner courtyard with a palm tree. And there were four other houses. Just four. Four drab little houses made of stone and mortar with tiled roofs and small windows. Ours. The one belonging to Skull's family. The one belonging to Remo's family, who shared it with old Tronca. Tronca was deaf and his wife had died, and he lived in two rooms overlooking the vegetable garden. And then there was the house of Pietro Mura, Barbara's father. Angela, his wife, had a shop on the ground floor where you could buy bread, pasta and soap. And you could make phone calls.

Two houses on one side, two on the other. And a road, rough and full of holes, in the middle. There was no piazza. There were no lanes. But there were two benches under a pergola of vines and a drinking fountain which had a tap so that water wouldn't be wasted. All around, the wheatfields.

The only thing of note in that place forgotten by God and man was a nice blue road sign which displayed in capital letters the words ACQUA TRAVERSE.

'Papa's home!' my sister shouted. She threw down her bike and ran up the steps.

Parked in front of our house was his truck, a Fiat Lupetto with a green tarpaulin.

At that time papa was working as a truck driver and would be away for weeks at a time. He collected the goods and carried them to the North.

He had promised he would take me with him to the North one day. I couldn't imagine this North very clearly. I knew the North was rich and the South was poor. And we were poor. Mama said that if papa kept working so hard, soon we wouldn't be poor any longer, we would be well off. So we mustn't complain if papa wasn't there. He was doing it for us.

I went into the house still out of breath.

Papa was sitting at the table in his vest and pants. He had a bottle of red wine in front of him and a cigarette in its holder between his lips and my sister perched on one thigh.

Mama, with her back to us, was cooking. There was a smell of onions and tomato sauce. The television, a big boxlike black-and-white Grundig, which papa had brought home a few months earlier, was on. The ventilator fan was humming.

'Michele, where've you been all day? Your mother was at her wits' end. Haven't you got any consideration for the poor woman? She's always having to wait for her husband, she shouldn't have to wait for you too. And what happened to your sister's glasses?'

He wasn't really angry. When he was really angry his eyes bulged like a toad's. He was happy to be home.

My sister looked at me.

'We built a hut by the stream.' I took the glasses out of my pocket. 'And they got broken.'

He spat out a cloud of smoke. 'Come over here. Let's see.'

Papa was a small man, thin and restless. When he sat in the driving seat of his truck he almost vanished behind the wheel. He had black hair, smoothed down with brilliantine. A rough white beard on his chin. He smelt of Nazionali and eau de cologne.

I gave him the glasses.

'They're a write-off.' He put them on the table and said, 'That's it. No more glasses.'

My sister and I looked at each other.

'What am I going to do?' she asked anxiously.

'Go without. That'll teach you.'

My sister was speechless.

'She can't. She can't see,' I interposed.

'Who cares?'

'But…'

'No buts.' And he said to mama, 'Teresa, give me that parcel on the kitchen cabinet.'

Mama brought it over. Papa unwrapped it and took out a hard velvety blue case. 'Here you are.'

Maria opened it and inside was a pair of glasses with brown plastic frames.

'Try them on.'

Maria put them on, but kept stroking the case.

Mama asked her: 'Do you like them?'

'Yes. They're lovely. The box is beautiful.' And she went to look at herself in the mirror.

Papa poured himself another glass of wine.

'If you break these, next time you'll go without, do you understand?' Then he took me by the arm. 'Let me feel that muscle.'

I bent my arm and stiffened it.

He squeezed my biceps. 'I don't think you've improved. Are you doing your press-ups?

'Yes.'

I hated doing press-ups. Papa wanted me to do them because he said I was puny.

'It's not true,' said Maria. 'He's not doing them.'

'I do them now and again. Almost always.'

'Come here.' I sat on his knee too and tried to kiss him. 'Don't you kiss me, you're all dirty. If you want to kiss your father, you've got to wash first. Teresa, what shall we do, send them to bed without supper?'

Papa had a nice smile, perfect white teeth. Neither my sister nor I has inherited them.

Mama replied without even turning round.

'It'd be no more than they deserve! I can't stand any more of these two.' *She* really was angry.

'Let's say this. If they want to have supper and get the present I've brought them, Michele's got to beat me at arm-wrestling. Otherwise, bed with no supper.'

He'd brought us a present!

'You and your jokes…' Mama was too happy that papa was home again. When papa went away her stomach hurt, and the more time passed the less she talked. After a month she went completely mute.

'Michele can't beat you. It's not fair,' said my sister.

'Michele, show your sister what you can do. And keep

those legs apart. If you sit crooked you'll lose straight away and there'll be no present.'

I got into position. I clenched my teeth and gripped papa's hand and started to push. Nothing. He didn't budge.

'Go on! Have you got ricotta instead of muscles? You're weaker than a gnat! Put your back into it, for God's sake!'

I murmured, 'I can't do it.'

It was like bending an iron bar.

'You're a sissy, Michele. Maria, help him, come on!'

My sister climbed on the table and together, gritting our teeth and breathing through our noses, we managed to get him to lower that arm.

'The present! Give us the present!' Maria jumped down from the table.

Papa picked up a cardboard box full of crumpled-up newspaper. Inside was the present.

'A boat!' I said.

'It's not a boat, it's a gondola,' papa explained.

'What's a gondola?'

'Gondolas are Venetian boats. They only use one oar.'

'What's an oar?' my sister asked.

'A stick to move a boat with.'

It was really beautiful. Made of black plastic. With little silvery pieces and at the end a little figure in a red-and-white striped shirt and a straw hat.

But we discovered that we weren't allowed to handle it. It was made to be put on the television. And between the television and the gondola there would have to be a white lace doily. Like a little lake. It wasn't a toy. It was something precious. An ornament.

'Whose turn is it to fetch the water? It'll be suppertime soon,' mama asked us.

Papa was in front of the television watching the news.

I was laying the table. 'It's Maria's turn', I said. 'I went yesterday.'

Maria was sitting in the armchair with her dolls. 'I don't feel like it, you go.'

Neither of us liked going to the drinking fountain so we took turns, one day each. But papa had come home and to my sister this meant the rules no longer applied.

I gestured no with my finger. 'It's your turn.'

Maria folded her arms. 'I'm not going.'

'Why not?'

'I've got a headache.'

Whenever she didn't want to do something she said she had a headache. It was her favourite excuse.

'It's not true, you haven't got a headache, liar.'

'Yes I have!' And she started massaging her forehead with a pained expression on her face.

I felt like throttling her. 'It's her turn! She's got to go!'

Mama, exasperated, put the jug in my hands. 'You go, Michele, you're the eldest. Don't make such a fuss.' She said it as if it was a trivial matter, something quite unimportant.

A smile of triumph spread on my sister's lips. 'See?'

'It's not fair. I went yesterday. I'm not going.'

Mama said to me with that harsh tone that came into her voice a moment before she lost her temper: 'Do as you're told, Michele.'

'No.' I went over to papa to complain. 'Papa, it's not my turn. I went yesterday.'

He took his eyes off the television and looked at me as

if it was the first time he had ever seen me, stroked his mouth and said, 'Do you know the soldier's draw?'

'No. What is it?'

'Do you know what the soldiers did during the war to decide who went on the dangerous missions?' He took a box of matches out of his pocket and showed it to me.

'No, I don't know.'

'You take three matches'—he took them out of the box—'one for you, one for me and one for Maria. You remove the head from one of them.' He took one and broke it, then he gripped them all in his fist and made the ends stick out. 'Whoever draws the headless match goes to get the water. Pick one, come on.'

I pulled out a whole one. I jumped for joy.

'Maria, it's your turn. Come on.'

My sister took a whole one too and clapped her hands.

'Looks like it's me.' Papa drew out the broken one.

Maria and I started laughing and shouting: 'You go! You go! You've lost! You've lost! Go and get the water!'

Papa got up, rather crestfallen. 'When I get back you must be washed. Do you hear me?'

'Would you like me to go? You're tired,' said mama.

'You can't. It's a dangerous mission. Besides, I've got to get my cigarettes from the truck.' And he went out of the house with the jug in his hand.

We got washed, ate pasta with tomato sauce and frittata, and after kissing papa and mama we went to bed without even begging to be allowed to watch television.

I woke up during the night. I had had a nightmare.

Jesus was telling Lazarus to rise and walk. But Lazarus didn't rise. Rise and walk, Jesus repeated. Lazarus just wouldn't come back to life. Jesus, who looked like Severino, the man who drove the water tanker, lost his temper. He was being made to look a fool. When Jesus tells you to rise and walk, you have to do it, especially if you're dead. But Lazarus just lay there, stiff as a board. So Jesus started shaking him like a doll and Lazarus finally rose up and bit him in the throat. Leave the dead alone, he said with blood-smeared lips.

I opened my eyes wide. I was covered in sweat.

Those nights it was so hot that if you were unfortunate enough to wake up it was hard to get back to sleep. The bedroom I shared with my sister was narrow and long. It had been converted from a corridor. The two beds were laid lengthwise, one after the other, under the window. On one side was the wall, on the other about thirty centimetres to move in. Otherwise the room was white and bare.

In winter it was cold and in summer you couldn't breathe.

The heat that was accumulated by the walls and ceiling in the daytime was emitted during the night. You felt as if your pillow and woollen mattress had come straight out of an oven.

Behind my feet I saw Maria's dark head. She was sleeping with her glasses on, face upwards, completely relaxed with her arms and legs apart.

She used to say that if she woke up without her glasses on she got scared. Usually mama took them off as soon as she fell asleep because they left marks on her face.

The insecticide coil on the windowsill produced a dense

toxic smoke that killed the mosquitoes and didn't do us much good either. But in those days nobody worried about that sort of thing.

Next to our room was our parents' room. I could hear papa snoring. The fan blowing. My sister panting. The monotonous hoot of a little owl. The buzz of the fridge. The stench of sewage from the toilet.

I knelt on the bed and leaned on the windowsill to get some air.

There was a full moon. It was high and bright. You could see for a long way, as if it were daytime. The fields seemed phosphorescent. The air was still. The houses dark, silent.

Maybe I was the only person awake in Acqua Traverse. It was a good feeling.

The boy was in the hole.

I imagined him dead in the earth. Cockroaches, bugs and millipedes crawling on him, over his bloodless skin, and worms coming out of his blue lips. His eyes were like two hard-boiled eggs.

I had never seen a dead body. Except my grandmother Giovanna. On her bed, with her arms crossed, in her black dress and shoes. Her face seemed to be made of rubber. Yellow like wax. Papa had told me I must kiss her. Everyone was crying. Papa was pushing me. I had put my lips on her cold cheek. It had a sickly sweet taste that mingled with the smell of the candles. Afterwards I had washed my lips with soap.

But what if the boy was alive?

If he wanted to get out and was scratching at the walls of the hole with his fingers and calling for help? If he had been caught by an ogre?

I looked out and far away on the plain I saw the hill. It seemed to have appeared out of nothing and stood up, like an island risen from the sea, tall and black, with its secret that was waiting for me.

'Michele, I'm thirsty…' Maria woke up. 'Will you get me a glass of water?' She was talking with her eyes closed and running her tongue over her dry lips.

'Just a minute…' I got up.

I didn't want to open the door. What if grandmother Giovanna was sitting at the table with the boy? Saying, come, sit down with us, let's eat? And there on the plate was the impaled hen?

There was nobody there. A ray of moonlight fell on the old flower-patterned sofa, on the kitchen cabinet with the white plates, and across the black-and-white tiled floor, and crept into my parents' bedroom, climbing up onto the bed. I saw their feet, intertwined. I opened the fridge and took out the jug of cold water. I took a swig from it, then filled a glass for my sister who drank it in one draught. 'Thank you.'

'Now go to sleep.'

'Why did you do the forfeit instead of Barbara?'

'I don't know…'

'Didn't you want her to pull down her knickers?'

'No.'

'What if I'd had to do it?'

'Do what?'

'Pull down my knickers. Would you have done it for me too?'

'Yes.'

'Good night, then. I'm going to take off my glasses.' She

40

shut them in their case and snuggled up to her pillow.

'Good night.'

I lay for a long time staring at the ceiling before I got back to sleep.

Papa wasn't going away again.

He had come home to stay. He had told mama he didn't want to see the autostrada again for a while and he was going to look after us.

Maybe, sooner or later, he would take us to the seaside for a swim.

WHEN I woke up mama and papa were still asleep. I gulped down some milk and some bread and marmalade, went out and got my bike.

'Where are you going?'

My sister was on the front steps, in her knickers, watching me.

'For a ride.'

'Where?'

'I don't know.'

'I want to come with you.'

'No.'

'I know where you're going…You're going on the mountain.'

'No I'm not. If mama and papa ask you anything, tell them I've gone for a ride and I won't be long.'

Another scorching day.

At eight o'clock in the morning the sun was still low but

was already beginning to roast the plain. I was going along the road we had come down the previous afternoon and wasn't thinking about anything, I was pedalling along amid the dust and insects trying to get there quickly. I took the road through the fields, the one that skirted the hill and led to the valley. Every now and then magpies rose from the wheat with their black and white tails. They chased each other, quarrelled, insulted each other with their raucous croaks. A hawk circled with still wings, drifting on the warm currents. I even saw a red hare, with long ears, dart across in front of me. I was finding it hard going, pushing on the pedals. The tyres slipped on the stones and the clods of dry earth. The closer I got to the house, the bigger the yellow hill grew in front of me, and the heavier the weight that crushed my chest, taking my breath away.

What if I arrived and found witches or an ogre there?

I knew witches met at night in abandoned houses and had parties and if you joined in you went mad and that ogres ate children.

I must be careful. If an ogre caught me, he would throw me in a hole too and eat me bit by bit. First an arm, then a leg and so on. And nobody would ever hear of me again. My parents would weep in despair. And everyone would say: 'Michele was such a nice boy, we're so sorry.' My aunts and uncles would come, and my cousin Evelina, in her blue Giulietta. Skull wouldn't cry, not him, nor would Barbara. My sister and Salvatore would, though.

I didn't want to die. Though I'd have liked to go to my funeral.

I didn't have to go up there. Was I out of my mind?

I turned my bike round and started for home. After a

hundred metres I braked.

What would Tiger Jack do in my place?

He wouldn't turn back even if Manitou in person ordered him to.

Tiger Jack.

Now there was a serious person. Tiger Jack, Tex Willer's Indian buddy.

And Tiger Jack would go up that hill even if an international conference of all the witches, bandits and ogres on the planet was taking place there, because he was a Navajo Indian, and he was fearless and invisible and silent as a puma and could climb and knew how to lie in wait for his enemies and then stab them with his knife.

I'm Tiger, even better, I'm Tiger's Italian son, I said to myself.

Pity I didn't have a knife, a bow or a Winchester.

I hid my bike, as Tiger would have done with his horse, ducked into the wheat and crawled forward on hands and knees, till my legs felt as stiff as pieces of wood and my arms were numb. Then I started hopping like a bird, looking right and left.

When I reached the valley I stopped for a few minutes to get my breath back, flattening against a tree trunk. And I flitted from tree to tree like a Sioux shadow. With my ears pricked up for any voice or suspicious sound. But all I heard was the blood throbbing in my eardrums.

Squatting behind a bush I scanned the house.

It was silent and still. Nothing seemed to have changed. If the witches had been there they had tidied up afterwards.

I squeezed through the brambles and found myself in the yard.

Hidden under the corrugated sheet and the mattress was the hole.

It hadn't been a dream.

I couldn't see him clearly. It was dark and full of flies and a sickening smell welled up.

I knelt on the edge.

'Are you alive?'

Nothing.

'Are you alive? Can you hear me?'

I waited, then I picked up a stone and threw it at him. It hit him on the foot. A thin, slender foot with black toes. A foot that didn't move a millimetre.

He was dead. And he would only get up from there if Jesus in person ordered him to.

My flesh crawled.

Dead dogs and cats had never affected me like this. Fur hides death. But this corpse, so white, with its arm thrown to one side, its head against the wall, was repulsive. There was no blood, nothing. Just a lifeless body in a dismal hole.

There was nothing human about him any more.

I must see his face. The face is the most important thing. From the face you can tell everything.

But going down there scared me. I could turn him over with a stick. It would take a pretty long one. I went into the cowshed and found a pole, but it was too short. I went back. A small, locked door gave on to the yard. I tried pushing it, but although it was rickety it held. Above the door there was a little window. I climbed up, supporting myself on the jambs, and got through head first. A couple of kilos heavier, or a bum like Barbara's, and I wouldn't have got through.

I found myself in the room I had seen while I was

crossing the bridge. There were the packets of pasta. The opened cans of tomatoes. Empty beer bottles. The remains of a fire. Some newspapers. A mattress. A drum full of water. A basket. I had the same feeling I had had the day before, that someone came here. This room wasn't disused like the rest of the house.

Under a grey blanket there was a big box. Inside I found a rope that ended in an iron hook.

With this I can get down, I thought.

I took it and chucked it through the little window and climbed out.

On the ground there was a rusty crane jib. I tied the rope round it. But I was afraid it would come undone and I would be left in the hole with the corpse. I tied three knots, like the ones papa tied on the tarpaulin of his truck. I pulled as hard as I could, it held. So I threw it into the hole.

'I'm not scared of anything,' I whispered to hearten myself, but my legs were wobbly and a voice in my brain was screaming at me not to go.

Dead people can't hurt you, I said to myself. I crossed myself and went down.

Inside it was colder.

The dead boy's skin was dirty, caked with mud and shit. He was naked. About the same height as me, but thinner. He was skin and bone. His ribs stuck out. He must be about my age.

I touched his hand with my toe, but it remained lifeless. I lifted the blanket that covered his legs. Round the right leg he had a big chain fastened with a padlock. The skin was scraped and raw. A thick transparent liquid oozed from the flesh and ran onto the rusty links of the chain, which was fixed to a buried ring.

I wanted to see his face. But I didn't want to touch his head. It gave me the creeps.

Finally, tentatively, I stretched out my arm and with two fingers took hold of one edge of the blanket and I was trying to lift it off his face when the dead boy bent his leg.

I clenched my fists and opened my mouth wide and terror gripped my testicles with an icy hand.

Then the dead boy raised his torso as if he was alive and with eyes closed stretched out his arms towards me.

My hair stood on end, I let out a yell, jumped backwards and tripped over the bucket and the shit spilled all over the place. I landed on my back screaming.

The dead boy started screaming too.

I thrashed about in the shit. Then at last with a desperate lunge I grabbed the rope and shot out of the hole like a flea gone berserk.

I pedalled, I swerved between holes and ruts at the risk of crashing, but I didn't slow down. My heart was exploding, my lungs were burning. I hit a bump and found myself in mid-air. I landed badly, I dragged one foot on the ground and squeezed the brakes, but that made it worse, the front wheel locked and I slid into the ditch at the side of the road. I got shakily back on my feet and looked at myself. One knee was grazed and bleeding, my T-shirt was spattered with shit, a leather strap on my sandal had snapped.

Breathe, I told myself.

I breathed and felt my heart calming down, my breathing returning to normal, and suddenly I felt sleepy. I lay down. I closed my eyes. Under my eyelids everything was red. The fear was still there, but it was just a slight burning way down in my stomach. The sun warmed my frozen arms. The crickets sang in my ears. My knee throbbed.

When I opened my eyes again some big black ants were crawling over me.

How long had I slept? It might have been five minutes or two hours.

I got on the Crock and rode on homewards. As I pedalled I kept seeing the dead boy rising up and stretching out his hands towards me. That gaunt face, those closed eyes, that open mouth, kept flashing in front of me.

Now it seemed to me like a dream. A bad dream that no longer had any force.

He was alive. He had pretended to be dead. Why?

Maybe he was ill. Maybe he was a monster.

A werewolf.

At night he became a wolf. They kept him chained up there because he was dangerous. I had seen a film on television about a man who changed into a wolf and attacked people whenever there was a full moon. The peasants set a trap and the wolf fell into it and a hunter shot it and the wolf died and turned back into a man. It was the pharmacist. And the hunter was the pharmacist's son.

They kept that boy chained up under a fibreglass sheet covered with earth so that he wouldn't be exposed to the moon's rays.

Werewolves can't be cured. To kill them you have

to have a silver bullet.

But werewolves didn't exist.

'Stop all this talk about monsters, Michele. Monsters don't exist. Ghosts, werewolves and witches are just nonsense invented to frighten mugs like you. It's men you should be afraid of, not monsters,' papa had said to me one day when I had asked him if monsters could breathe underwater.

But if they had hidden him there, there must be a reason.

Papa would explain it all to me.

'Papa! Papa!…' I pushed the door and rushed in. 'Papa! I've got something to…' The rest died on my lips.

He was sitting in the armchair with the newspaper in his hands looking at me with toad's eyes. The worst toad's eyes I had seen since the day I had drunk the Lourdes water thinking it was acqua minerale. He squashed his cigarette-end in his coffee cup.

Mama was sitting on the sofa sewing, she raised her head and lowered it again.

Papa drew in air through his nose and said, 'Where have you been all day?' He looked me up and down. 'Have you seen yourself? What the hell have you been rolling in?' He grimaced. 'Shit? You stink like a pig! And you've broken your sandals too!' He looked at the clock. 'Do you know what time it is?'

I said nothing.

'I'll tell you. Twenty past three. You didn't turn up for lunch. Nobody knew where you were. I went all the way to Lucignano looking for you. Yesterday you got away with it. Not today.'

When he was so furious papa didn't shout, he spoke in a low voice. That terrified me. Even today I can't stand people who don't give vent to their anger.

He pointed towards the door. 'If you want to do as you please, you'd better go away. I don't want you. Get out.'

'Wait a minute, I've got something to tell you.'

'I don't want to hear it, I just want you to go out through that door.'

I pleaded. 'Papa, it's important…'

'If you're not out of here in three seconds I'm going to get up from this chair and kick you all the way to the Acqua Traverse road sign.' And suddenly he raised his voice: 'Get out!'

I nodded. I felt like crying. My eyes filled with tears, I opened the door and went down the steps. I got on the Crock again and cycled down to the stream.

The stream was always dry, except in winter, when it rained hard. It wound its way between the yellow fields like a long albino snake. A bed of white pointed stones, incandescent rocks and tufts of grass. After a steep part between two hills, the stream widened out to form a pond which in summer dried up into a black puddle.

The lake, we called it.

There were no fish in it, nor tadpoles, only mosquito larvae and water boatmen. If you put your feet in it, you took them out covered in dark, stinking mud.

We went there for the carob.

It was big, old and easy to climb. We dreamed of
building a tree house on it. With a door, a roof, a rope ladder
and all the rest. But we had never been able to find the
planks, the nails, or the skill. Once Skull had fixed a
bedspring up there. But it was very uncomfortable. It
scratched you. Tore your clothes. And if you moved too
much you were liable to fall out.

Lately the others had stopped climbing the carob. I still
liked it, though. I felt good up there in the shade, hidden
among the leaves. You could see a long way, it was like being
at the top of a ship's mast. Acqua Traverse was a tiny patch,
a dot lost in the wheat. And you could keep watch over the
Lucignano road. From there I could see the green tarpaulin
of papa's truck before anybody else.

I climbed up to my usual place, astride a thick branch
that forked out, and decided I would never go home again.

If papa didn't want me, if he hated me, I didn't care, I
would stay there. I could live without a family, like the
orphans.

'I don't want you. Get out.'

All right, I said to myself. But when I don't come back
you'll be sorry. And then you'll come under the tree and
ask me to come back but I won't come back and you'll beg
me and I won't come back and you'll realise you were wrong
and your son won't come back and he lives on the carob.

I took off my T-shirt, rested my back against the wood,
my head in my hands, and looked at the hill where the boy
was. It was far away, at the end of the plain, and the sun
was setting beside it. It was an orange disc that faded to
pink against the clouds and the sky.

'Michele, come down!'

I woke up and opened my eyes.

Where was I?

It took me a few moments to realise I was perched on the carob.

'Michele!'

Under the tree, on her Graziella, was Maria. I yawned. 'What do you want?' I stretched. My back was all stiff.

She got off her bike. 'Mama said you've got to come home.'

I put my T-shirt on again. It was beginning to get cold. 'No, I'm not coming home, tell her. I'm staying here!'

'Mama said supper's ready.'

It was late. There was still a bit of light but in half an hour it would be dark. I wasn't too happy about that.

'Tell them I'm not their son any more and you're their only child.'

My sister frowned. 'And you're not my brother either?'

'No.'

'So I can have the room to myself and I can have all your comics?'

'No, that's got nothing to do with it.'

'Mama says if you don't come, she will. And she'll spank you.' She beckoned me down.

'I don't care. Anyway, she can't get up the tree.'

'Yes she can. Mama'll climb up.'

'Well, I'll throw stones at her.'

She got on her saddle. 'She'll be cross, you know.'

'Where's papa?'

'He's not there.'

'Where is he?'

'He's gone out. He won't be back till late.'

'Where's he gone?'

'I don't know. Are you coming?'

I was starving. 'What's for supper?'

'Purée and eggs,' she said as she rode off.

Purée and eggs. I loved both of them. Especially when I stirred them together and they became a delicious mush.

I jumped down from the carob. 'All right, I'll come. Just for this evening, though.'

At supper nobody talked.

It was as if there had been a death in the family. My sister and I ate sitting at the table.

Mama was washing the dishes. 'When you've finished go straight to bed and no grumbling.'

'What about the television?' Maria asked.

'No television. Your father'll be back soon and if he finds you up there'll be trouble.'

I asked, 'Is he still very cross?'

'Yes.'

'What did he say?'

'He said if you go on like this, next year he'll take you to the friars.'

Whenever I did anything wrong papa always threatened to send me to the friars.

Salvatore and his mother went to the monastery of San Biagio now and then because his uncle was the friar guardian. One day I had asked Salvatore what it was like there.

'Lousy,' he had replied. 'You spend all day praying and

in the evening they shut you up in a room and if you need a pee you can't do it and they make you wear sandals even if it's cold.'

I hated the friars, but I knew I would never go there because papa hated them even more than I did and said they were pigs.

I put my plate in the sink. 'Won't papa ever get over it?'

'If he finds you asleep he might,' Mama said.

Mama never sat at table with us.

She served us and ate standing up. With her plate resting on the fridge. She spoke little and stayed on her feet. She was always on her feet. Cooking. Washing. Ironing. If she wasn't on her feet, she was asleep. The television bored her. When she was tired she flopped on her bed and went out like a light.

At the time of this story mama was thirty-three. She was still beautiful. She had long black hair that reached halfway down her back and she let it hang loose. She had two dark eyes as big as almonds, a wide mouth, strong white teeth and a pointed chin. She looked Arabian. She was tall, shapely, she had a big bosom, a narrow waist and a bottom that made you long to touch it and wide hips.

When we went to the market in Lucignano I saw how the men's eyes would be glued to her. I saw the fruit-seller nudge the man on the next stall and they looked at her bottom and then raised their heads to the sky. I held her hand, I clutched onto her skirt.

She's mine, leave her alone, I felt like shouting.

'Teresa, you give a man evil thoughts,' said Severino,

the guy who brought the water tanker.

Mama wasn't interested in these things. She didn't see them. Those lecherous looks just slipped off her. Those peeks into the V of her dress left her cold.

She was no flirt.

It was so humid you couldn't breathe. We were in bed. In the dark.

'Do you know an animal that starts with a fruit?' my sister asked me.

'What?'

'An animal that starts with a fruit.'

I started thinking about it. 'Do you know?'

'Yes.'

'Who told you?'

'Barbara.'

I couldn't think of anything. 'There's no such thing.'

'Yes there is, yes there is.'

I had a stab. 'A plumber.'

'That's not an animal. It doesn't count.'

My mind was a blank. I ran through all the fruit I knew and stuck bits of animals on the end but nothing came of it.

'A peachinese?'

'No.'

'A pearanha?'

'No.'

'I don't know. I give up. What is it?'

'I'm not telling you.'

'You've got to tell me now.'

'All right, I'll tell you. An orang-utan.'

I slapped myself on the forehead. 'Of course! An orange utan! It was dead easy. What a fool…'

'Good night,' said Maria.

'Good night,' I replied.

I tried to sleep, but I wasn't sleepy, I tossed and turned in bed.

I looked out of the window. The moon was no longer a perfect ball and there were stars everywhere. That night the boy couldn't turn into a wolf. I looked towards the mountain. And for an instant I thought a light was glimmering on the top.

I wondered what was happening in the abandoned house.

Maybe the witches were there, naked and old, standing round the hole laughing toothlessly and maybe they were dragging the boy out of the hole and making him dance and pulling his pecker. Maybe the ogre and the gypsies were there cooking him on hot coals.

I wouldn't have gone up there at night for all the tea in China. I wished I could turn into a bat and fly over the house. Or put on the old suit of armour that Salvatore's father kept by the front door and go up onto the hill. Wearing that I would be safe from the witches.

IN THE morning I woke up calm, I hadn't had nightmares. I stayed in bed for a while, with my eyes closed, listening to the birds. Then I started seeing the boy rising up and stretching out his arms again.

'Help!' I said.

What an idiot I was! That's why he had sat up. He had been asking me for help and I had run away.

I went out of the room in my underpants. Papa was tightening the coffee pot. Barbara's father was sitting at the table.

They turned round.

'Good morning,' said papa. He wasn't angry any more.

'Hello Michele,' said Barbara's father. 'How are you?'

'Fine.'

Pietro Mura was a short, stocky man, with a big black moustache that covered his mouth and a square head. He was wearing a black suit with thin white stripes and a vest. He had been a barber in Lucignano for a number of years, but business had never been good and when a new salon had opened with manicuring and modern hairstyles he had shut up shop and now he was a small farmer. But in Acqua Traverse he was still known as the barber.

If you needed a haircut you went round to his house. He would sit you down in the kitchen, in the sun, next to the cage with the goldfinches in it, open a drawer and take out a rolled-up cloth in which he kept his combs and his well-oiled scissors.

Pietro Mura had short thick fingers like toscano cigars that barely fitted into the scissors, and before he started cutting he would open the blades and pass them over your head, in front and behind, like a water diviner. He said that when he did this he could feel your thoughts, whether they were good or bad.

And I, when he did this, used to try and think only of nice things like ice-creams, falling stars or how much I loved mama.

He looked at me and said, 'What're you trying to be, a longhair?'

I shook my head.

Papa poured the coffee into the good cups.

'He drove me up the wall yesterday. If he carries on like this I'm sending him to the friars.'

The barber asked me, 'Do you know how friars have their hair cut?'

'With a hole in the middle.'

'That's right. You'd better be good then.'

'Come on, get dressed and have breakfast,' said papa. 'Mama's left you the bread and milk.'

'Where's she gone?'

'To Lucignano. To the market.'

'Papa, I've got something to tell you. Something important.'

He put on his jacket. 'You can tell me this evening. I'm going out. Wake up your sister and warm the milk.' In one gulp he downed his coffee.

The barber drank his and they both went out of the house.

After getting Maria's breakfast I went down into the street.

Skull and the others were playing soccer in the sun.

Togo, a little black and white mongrel, was chasing the ball and getting under everyone's feet.

Togo had appeared in Acqua Traverse at the beginning of the summer and had been adopted by the whole village. He had made himself a bed in Skull's father's shed. Everybody gave him leftovers and he had become a great fat thing with a stomach swollen like a drum. He was a nice little dog. When you stroked him or took him indoors he became excited and squatted down and peed.

'You go in goal,' Salvatore shouted to me.

I went. Nobody else liked being goalkeeper. I did. Maybe because I was better with my hands than with my feet. I liked jumping, diving, rolling in the dust. Saving penalties.

The others just wanted to score goals.

I let in a hatful that morning. Either I fumbled the ball or I was late getting down to it. My mind was elsewhere.

Salvatore came over to me. 'What's the matter, Michele?'

'The matter?'

'You're playing terribly.'

I spat on my hands, spread my arms and legs and narrowed my eyes like Zoff.

'Now I'll save it. I'll save everything.'

Skull beat Remo and fired in a hard direct shot. It was well struck, but an easy one, the sort you can punch away one-handed or clutch to your stomach. I tried to grab it but it slipped through my hands.

'Goal!' roared Skull and punched the air as if he had scored against Juventus.

The hill was calling me. I could go. Papa and mama were out. As long as I was back by lunchtime.

'I'm not in the mood for football,' I said and went off.

Salvatore ran after me. 'Where are you going?'

'Nowhere.'

'Shall we go for a ride?'

'Later. There's something I have to do now.'

I had run away and left everything like this: the corrugated sheet thrown to one side with the mattress, the hole uncovered and the rope hanging down inside.

If the guardians of the hole had come, they must have seen that their secret had been discovered and they would get me.

What if he wasn't there any more?

I must pluck up courage and look.

I leaned over.

He was rolled up in the blanket.

I cleared my throat. 'Hi…Hi…Hi…I'm the boy who came yesterday. I came down, remember?'

No reply.

'Can you hear me? Are you deaf?' It was a stupid question. 'Are you ill? Are you alive?'

He bent his arm, raised his hand and whispered something.

'What? I didn't catch that.'

'Water.'

'Water? Are you thirsty?'

He raised his arm.

'Wait a minute.'

Where was I going to find water? There were a couple of paint buckets, but they were empty. In the washing trough there was a little water, but it was green and crawling with mosquito larvae.

I remembered that when I had gone in to get the rope I had seen a drum full of water.

'I'll be right back,' I said, and climbed through the little window over the door.

The drum was half full, but the water was clear and didn't smell. It seemed all right.

In a dark corner, on a wooden plank, there were some cans, some half-burned candles, a saucepan and some empty bottles. I took one bottle, walked two paces and stopped. I went back and picked up the saucepan.

It was a shallow pan covered in white enamel, with a blue rim and handles, and red apples painted round the outside. It was just like the one we had at home. We had bought ours with mama at Lucignano market, Maria had chosen it from a pile of saucepans on a stall because she liked the apples.

This one looked older. It hadn't been properly washed, there was still some stuff stuck on the bottom. I ran my forefinger over it and brought it up to my nose.

Tomato sauce.

I put it back and filled the bottle with water, closing it with a cork stopper, took the basket and climbed out.

I grabbed the rope, tied the basket to it and put the bottle inside.

'I'll lower it down to you,' I said. 'Take it.'

With the blanket round him, he groped for the bottle in the basket, uncorked it and poured the water into the saucepan without spilling a drop, then he put it back in the basket and gave a tug on the cord.

As if it was something he always did, every day. Since I didn't take it back he gave a second tug and grunted something angrily.

As soon as I had pulled it up he lowered his head and without lifting the saucepan started to drink, on all fours, like a dog. When he had finished he crouched down on one side and didn't move again.

It was late.

'Well…goodbye.' I covered up the hole and went away.

While I was cycling towards Acqua Traverse, I thought about the saucepan I had found in the kitchen.

I found it strange that it was the same as ours. I don't know why, maybe because Maria had chosen it from so many. As if it was special, more beautiful, with those red apples.

I arrived home just in time for lunch.

'Hurry up, go and wash your hands,' said papa. He was sitting at the table next to my sister. They were waiting for mama to drain the pastasciutta.

I dashed into the bathroom and rubbed my hands with

the soap, parted my hair on the right and joined them while mama was filling the plates with pasta.

She wasn't using the saucepan with the apples on it. I looked at the dishes drying on the sink, but I couldn't see it there either. It must be in the kitchen cabinet.

'In a couple of days somebody's coming to stay with us,' said papa with his mouth full. 'You must both be good. No crying and shouting. Don't show me up.'

'Who is this somebody?' I asked.

He poured himself a glass of wine. 'A friend of mine.'

'What's his name?' my sister asked.

'Sergio.'

'Sergio,' Maria repeated. 'What a funny name.'

It was the first time anyone had ever come to stay with us. At Christmas my uncles and aunts came but they hardly ever stayed the night. There wasn't enough room. I asked, 'And how long is he staying?'

Papa filled his plate again. 'For a while.'

Mama put the little slice of meat in front of us.

It was Wednesday. And Wednesday was meat day.

The meat that's good for you, the meat my sister and I couldn't stand. I, with a great effort, could get that tough tasteless bit of shoe-leather down, but my sister couldn't. She would chew it for hours till it became a stringy white ball that swelled up in her mouth. And when she really couldn't stand it any more she would stick it on the underside of the table. There the meat fermented. Mama just couldn't understand it. 'Where's that smell coming from? What on earth can it be?' Till one day she took out the cutlery drawer and found all those ghastly pellets stuck to the boards like wasps' nests.

But now the trick had been rumbled.

Maria started moaning. 'I don't want it! I don't like it!'

Mama lost her temper at once. 'Maria, eat up that meat!'

'I can't. It gives me a headache,' my sister said as if they were offering her poison.

Mama gave her a sharp slap on the head and Maria started whimpering.

Now she'll get sent to bed, I thought.

But papa picked up the plate and looked mama in the eyes. 'Leave her alone, Teresa. So she won't eat it. It doesn't matter. Put it away.'

After lunch my parents went to have a rest. The house was an oven, but they managed to sleep anyway.

It was the right moment to search for the saucepan. I opened the kitchen cabinet and rummaged through the crockery. I looked in the chest of drawers where we put the things that weren't used any more. I went outside and looked behind the house where the washing trough, the vegetable garden and the clotheslines were. Sometimes mama washed the dishes out there and left them to dry in the sun.

Nothing. The saucepan with the apples had disappeared.

We were sitting under the pergola playing spit-in-the-ocean and waiting for the sun to go down a bit so we could have a game of football, when I saw papa going down the steps, wearing his good trousers and a clean shirt. He was carrying a blue bag that I had never seen before.

Maria and I got up and reached him as he was getting into the truck.

'Papa, papa, where are you going? Are you going away?' I asked him, clinging on to the door.

'Can we come with you?' begged my sister.

A nice ride in the truck was just what the doctor ordered. We both remembered when he had taken us to eat rustici and cream pastries.

He turned on the ignition. 'Sorry kids. Not today.'

I tried to get into the cab. 'But you said you wouldn't go away again, you'd stay at home…'

'I'll be back soon. Tomorrow or the day after. Out you get, now.' He was in a hurry. He wasn't in the mood to argue.

My sister tried pleading with him a little longer. I didn't, there was no point.

We watched him depart in the dust, at the wheel of his great green box.

I woke up during the night.

And not because of a dream. Because of a noise.

I lay there, with my eyes closed, listening.

I seemed to be on the sea. I could hear it. Except that it was a sea of iron, a lazy ocean of bolts, screws and nails that lapped on a beach. Slow waves of scrap crashed in heavy breakers that covered and uncovered the shoreline.

Mingled with that sound were the howls and despairing yelps of a pack of dogs, a mournful tuneless chorus that didn't allay the noise of the iron but increased it.

I looked out of the window. A combine harvester was

clattering along the moonlit crest of a hill. It was like a huge metal grasshopper, with two bright round little eyes and a wide mouth made of blades and spikes. A mechanical insect that devoured wheat and shitted out straw. It worked by night because in the daytime it was too hot. That was what was making the sound of the sea.

And I knew where the howls were coming from.

From Skull's father's kennels. Italo Natale had built a corrugated iron hut behind his house and kept his hounds locked up there. They were always in there, summer and winter, behind wire netting. When Skull's father took them their food in the morning they barked.

That night, for some reason, they had all started howling together.

I looked towards the hill.

Papa was there. He had taken my sister's meat to the boy and that was why he had pretended to be going away and that was why he had a bag, to hide it in.

Before supper I had opened the fridge and the meat wasn't there any more.

'Mama, where's that slice of meat?'

She had looked at me in amazement. 'Do you like meat now?'

'Yes.'

'It's not there. Your father's eaten it.'

No he hadn't. He had taken it for the boy.

Because the boy was my brother.

Like Nunzio Scardaccione, Salvatore's big brother. Nunzio wasn't a bad lunatic, but I couldn't bear to look at him. I was scared he would infect me with his madness. Nunzio tore out his hair with his hands and ate it. His head was all pits and scabs and he dribbled. His mother put a hat and gloves on him so he wouldn't tear his hair out, but he had started biting his arms till they bled. In the end they had taken him and carried him off to the mental hospital. I had been glad.

Maybe the boy in the hole was my brother, and he had been born mad like Nunzio and papa had hidden him there, so as not to frighten my sister and me. Not to frighten the children of Acqua Traverse.

Maybe he and I were twins. We were the same height and we seemed to be the same age.

When we were born, mama had taken both of us from the cradle, she had sat on a chair and put her breasts in our mouths to give us milk. I had started to suck but he had bitten her nipple, tried to tear it off, the blood and milk was dripping from her tit and mama shouted round the house, 'He's crazy! He's crazy! Pino, take him away! Take him away! Kill him, he's crazy.'

Papa had put him in a sack and taken him onto the hill to kill him, he had put him on the ground, in the wheat, and he should have stabbed him but he couldn't bring himself to do it, he was his son after all, so he had dug a hole, chained him inside and brought him up there.

Mama didn't know he was alive.

I did.

I WOKE up early. I stayed in bed while the sun began to glow. Then I couldn't bear to wait any longer. Mama and Maria were still asleep. I got up, cleaned my teeth, filled my schoolbag with some cheese and bread and went out.

I had decided that in the daytime there was no danger on the hill, it was only at night that nasty things happened.

That morning the clouds had appeared. They ran swiftly across a faded sky throwing black patches on the wheatfields and clung on to their rain, carrying it off somewhere else.

I raced across the deserted countryside, on the Crock, heading for the house.

If I found even a scrap of the meat in the hole it would mean the boy was my brother.

I was nearly there when a thick red dust cloud appeared on the horizon. Low. Fast. A cloud advancing in the wheat. The sort of cloud that can be raised by a car on a sun-baked earth track. It was a long way off but it wouldn't take long to reach me. I could already hear the drone of its engine.

It was coming from the abandoned house. That was the only place the road led to. A car curved slowly round and came straight towards me.

I didn't know what to do. If I turned back it would catch up with me, if I went on they would see me. I must decide quickly, it was getting closer. Maybe they had already seen me. If they hadn't it was only because of the red cloud they were raising.

I turned my bike round and started to pedal, trying to get away as fast I could. It was no good. The more I pushed on the pedals, the more the bike jibbed, swayed and refused to go forward. I looked round, and behind me the dust cloud was growing.

Hide, I told myself.

I swerved, the bike reared up on a stone and I flew like a crucifix into the wheat. The car was less than two hundred metres away.

The Crock was lying at the edge of the road. I grabbed the front wheel and dragged it over beside me. I flattened down on the ground. Not breathing. Not moving a muscle. Asking Baby Jesus not to let them see me.

Baby Jesus granted my request.

Lying among the stalks, with the horseflies feasting on my skin and my hands dug into the burning clods, I saw a brown 127 shoot past.

Felice Natale's 127.

Felice Natale was Skull's big brother. If Skull was bad, Felice was a thousand times worse.

Felice was twenty. And whenever he was in Acqua

Traverse life was hell for me and the other children. He would hit us, puncture our football and steal things from us.

He was a poor devil. Friendless, womanless. A guy who bullied children, a soul in torment. And that was understandable. No twenty-year-old could live in Acqua Traverse without ending up like Nunzio Scardaccione, the hair-tearer. Felice in Acqua Traverse was like a tiger in a cage. He paced around among that tiny group of houses, furious, restless, ready to pick on you. It was lucky he went off to Lucignano now and again. But even there he hadn't made any friends. When I came out of school I used to see him sitting alone on a bench in the piazza.

That year the fashion was flared trousers, tight-fitting brightly coloured T-shirts, sheepskin coats and long hair. Not Felice—he had his hair cut short and combed it back with brilliantine, he shaved perfectly and wore combat jackets and camouflaged trousers. And he tied a bandanna round his neck. He drove around in that 127, he liked guns and said he had been in the parachute regiment at Pisa and had jumped out of planes. But it wasn't true. Everyone knew he had done his military service at Brindisi. He had the pointed face of a barracuda and little gappy teeth like a baby crocodile's. Once he had told us they were like that because they were still his milk teeth. He had never changed them. As long as he didn't open his mouth he was almost good-looking, but if he opened up, if he laughed, you took two steps backwards. And if he caught you looking at his teeth you were for it.

Then, one blessed day, without saying a word to anyone, he had left.

If you asked Skull where his brother had gone he would reply, 'To the North. To work.'

That was all we wanted to know.

But now he had popped up again like a poisonous weed. In his diarrhoea-coloured 127. And he was coming down from the abandoned house.

He had put the boy in the hole. That was who had put him there.

Hidden among the trees, I checked that there was nobody in the valley.

When I was sure I was alone, I came out of the wood and climbed into the house through the usual window. As well as the packets of pasta, the bottles of beer and the saucepan with the apples, on the floor there were a couple of opened cans of tuna. And on one side, rolled up, was an army sleeping bag.

Felice. It was his. I could just see him, sheathed in his sleeping bag, happily guzzling the tuna.

I filled a bottle with water, got the rope out of the box and took it outside. I tied it to the crane jib, moved the corrugated sheet and mattress and looked down.

He was curled up like a hedgehog in the brown blanket.

I didn't want to go down there, but I had to find out if there were any remains of my sister's slice of meat. Even though I had seen Felice coming from the hill I couldn't get it out of my head that the boy might be my brother.

I took out the cheese and asked him, 'Can I come down? I'm the one who gave you the water. Do you remember? I've brought you something to eat. Caciotta. It's good, caciotta. Better, ten times better, than meat. If you don't attack me, I'll give it to you.'

He didn't reply.

'Well, can I come down?'

Maybe Felice had cut his throat.

'I'll throw the caciotta down. Catch it.' I threw it to him. It landed near him.

A black hand, quick as a tarantula, shot out of the blanket and started to feel about on the ground till it found the cheese, grabbed it and whipped it back underneath. While he was eating his legs quivered, like those stray dogs when they come across a bit of leftover steak after days without food.

'I've got some water too…shall I bring it down?'

He made a gesture with his arm.

I let myself down.

As soon as he felt I was near him, he cowered back against the wall.

I looked around, there was no trace of the meat.

'I won't hurt you. Are you thirsty?' I held out the bottle. 'Drink it, it's good.'

He sat up without taking off the blanket. He looked like a ragged little ghost. His thin legs stuck out like two spindly white twigs. One was chained up. He put out an arm and snatched the bottle from me and, like the cheese, it vanished under the blanket.

The ghost acquired a long anteater's nose. He was drinking.

He drained it in twenty seconds. And when he had finished, he even gave a burp.

'What's your name?' I asked him.

He curled up again without deigning to reply.

'What's your father's name?'

I waited in vain.

'My father's name's Pino, what's yours? Is your father called Pino too?'

He seemed to be asleep.

I stood looking at him, then I said, 'Felice! Do you know him? I saw him. He was driving down in his car...' I didn't know what else to say. 'Do you want me to go? If you want I'll go.' Nothing. 'All right, I'll go.' I grabbed the rope. 'Goodbye, then...'

I heard a whisper, a breath, something came out of the blanket.

I moved closer. 'Did you speak?'

He whispered again.

'I don't understand. Speak louder.'

'The little bears...!' he shouted.

I jumped. 'The little bears? What do you mean, the little bears?'

He lowered his voice. 'The little wash-bears...'

'The little wash-bears?'

'The little wash-bears. If you leave the kitchen window open the little wash-bears come in and steal the cakes or the biscuits, depending on what you're eating that day,' he said very seriously. 'If you, for example, leave the rubbish in front of the house, the little wash-bears come in the night and eat it up.'

He was like a broken radio that had suddenly started transmitting again.

'It's very important to shut the bucket properly, other-wise they'll spill everything out.'

What was he talking about? I tried to interrupt him. 'There aren't any bears here. Nor wolves. There are some foxes.' And then I asked him, 'Did you by any chance have a slice of meat yesterday?'

'The little wash-bears bite because they're scared of humans.'

Who the hell were these little wash-bears? And what did they wash? Clothes? Besides, bears only talk in comics. I didn't like this little wash-bear business…

I persisted. 'Could you please tell me if you had a slice of meat yesterday? It's very important.'

And he replied: 'The little bears told me you're not scared of the lord of the worms.'

A little voice in my brain was saying I mustn't listen to him, I must run away.

I grasped the rope, but I couldn't bring myself to leave, I kept staring at him spellbound.

He persisted. 'You're not scared of the lord of the worms.'

'The lord of the worms? Who's he?'

'The lord of the worms says, Hey, little sap! I'm going to send down the stuff now. Take it and give me back the bucket. Otherwise I'll come down and squash you like a worm. Yeah, squash you like a worm, I will. Are you the guardian angel?'

'What?'

'Are you the guardian angel?'

I stammered, 'I…I, no…I'm not the angel…'

'You *are* the angel. You've got the same voice.'

'What angel?'

'The one that talks, that says things.'

'Isn't it the little wash-bears that talk?' I couldn't make any sense of these ravings. 'You told me so…'

'The little bears talk, but sometimes they tell lies. The angel always tells the truth. You're the guardian angel.' He raised his voice. 'You can tell me.'

I felt weak. The smell of shit stopped up my mouth, my nose, my brain. 'I'm not an angel…I'm Michele, Michele Amitrano. I'm not a…' I murmured and leaned against the wall and slid down to the ground and he got up, stretched out his arms towards me like a leper asking for alms and he stayed up for a few moments, then took one step and fell down, on his knees, under the blanket, at my feet.

He touched one of my fingers, whispering.

I let out a yell. As if I had been touched by a disgusting jellyfish, a venomous spider. With that bony little hand, with those long black twisted nails of his.

He was speaking too quietly. 'What, what did you say?'

'What did you say? I'm dead!' he replied.

'What?'

'What? Am I dead? Am I dead? I'm dead. What?'

'Speak louder. Louder…Please…'

He gave a hoarse, voiceless scream, as piercing as a fingernail on a blackboard. 'Am I dead? Am I dead? I'm dead.'

I fumbled for the rope and pulled myself up, kicking out and knocking earth down on him.

But he kept shrieking. 'Am I dead? I'm dead. Am I dead?'

I pedalled along pursued by horseflies.

And I swore I would never, never go back onto that hill. Never, even if they blinded me, would I speak to that lunatic again.

How on earth could he think he was dead?

Nobody who's alive can think they're dead. When you're dead, you're dead. And you live in heaven. Or maybe in hell.

But what if he was right?

If he really was dead? If they had brought him back to life? Who? Only Jesus Christ can bring you back to life. And no one else. But when you wake up do you know you've been dead? Do you remember about heaven? Do you remember who you were before? You go mad, because your brain has rotted and you start talking about little wash-bears.

He wasn't my twin and he wasn't even my brother. And papa had nothing to do with him. The slice of meat had nothing to do with him. The saucepan wasn't ours. Mama had thrown ours away.

And as soon as papa came back I would tell him the whole story. As he had taught me. And he would do something.

I had almost reached the road when I remembered the corrugated sheet. I had run away and left the hole open again.

If Felice went back up he would know at once that someone had been there poking his nose where he shouldn't poke it. I couldn't let myself get caught just because I was scared of a loony chained up in a hole. If Felice found out it had been me, he would drag me around by the ear.

Once, Skull and I had got into Felice's car. We pretended the 127 was a spaceship. He drove and I shot at the Martians. Felice had caught us and yanked us out, in the middle of the road, pulling us by the ears, like rabbits. We cried our eyes out but he wouldn't stop. Luckily mama had come out and given him a thrashing.

I wished I could leave everything like that, run home and shut myself up in my bedroom and read comics, but I turned back, cursing myself. The clouds had gone and it was scorching hot. I took off my T-shirt and tied it round my head, like an Indian. I picked up a stick. If I met Felice I would defend myself.

I tried not to get any nearer than necessary to the hole, but I couldn't resist looking.

He was kneeling under the blanket with his arm stretched out, in the same position I had left him in.

I felt like jumping on that damned sheet and breaking it in a thousand pieces, but instead I pushed it and covered the hole.

When I got home mama was washing the dishes. She threw the frying pan in the sink. 'Well, well, look who's back!'

She was so angry her jaw was quivering. 'Where on earth do you get to? You gave me the fright of my life…The other day your father didn't give you a spanking. But this time you're going to get one.'

I didn't even have time to think up an excuse before she started chasing me. I jumped from one side of the kitchen to the other like a goat while my sister, sitting at the table, watched me, shaking her head.

'Where are you going? Come here!'

I dived behind the sofa, crawled under the table, clambered over the armchair, slithered along the floor into my bedroom and hid under the bed.

'Come out of there!'

'No. You'll smack me!'

'I certainly will. If you come out of your own accord you'll get fewer smacks.'

'No, I'm not coming out!'

'Very well then.'

A vice clamped on my ankle. I grabbed hold of the leg of the bed with both hands, but it was no use. Mama was stronger than Superman and that damned iron claw was slipping through my fingers. I let go and found myself between her legs. I tried to crawl back under the bed, but she didn't give me a chance, she pulled me up by the trousers and tucked me under her arm as if I was a suitcase.

I screamed. 'Let me go! Please! Let me go!'

She sat on the sofa, put me over her knees, pulled down my trousers and pants while I bleated like a lamb, threw back her hair and started to tan my backside.

Mama always had heavy hands. Her spanks were slow and well-aimed and made a dull thud, like a carpet beater on a rug.

'I was looking for you everywhere.' One. 'Nobody knew where you'd got to.' Two. 'You'll be the death of me.' Three. 'They must have thought I'm a bad mother.' Four. 'And that I don't know how to bring up kids.'

'Stop!' I shouted. 'Stop! Please, please, mama!'

On the radio a voice sang: '*Croce. Croce e delizia. Delizia al cor.*'

I remember it as if it were yesterday. All my life, whenever I've listened to *La Traviata*, I've seen myself lying with my bottom in the air, over my mother's knee, as she sat straight-backed on the sofa, beating the living daylights out of me.

'What shall we do?' Salvatore asked me.

We were sitting on the bench throwing stones at an old boiler that had been dumped in the wheat. If you hit it you scored a point. The others, at the end of the street, were playing hide-and-seek.

The day had been windy, but now, at dusk, the air had calmed, it was sultry, and a band of weary bluish clouds had settled behind the fields.

I threw too far. 'I don't know. I can't go cycling, my bum hurts. My mother smacked me.'

'Why?'

'Because I'm always coming home late. Does your mother smack you?'

Salvatore threw and hit the boiler with a good bang. 'Point! Three—one.' Then he shook his head. 'No. She can't. She's too fat.'

'You're lucky. My mother's really strong and she can run faster than a bike.'

He laughed. 'That's impossible.'

I picked up a smaller stone and hurled it. This time I nearly hit the target. 'I swear. Once, in Lucignano, we had to catch the bus. When we got there, it was just moving off. Mama ran after it so fast she caught up with it and started thumping on the door. They stopped.'

'If my mother tried to run she'd die.'

'Listen,' I said. 'Do you remember when Signorina Destani told us the story of the miracle of Lazarus?'

'Yes.'

'Do you reckon Lazarus knew he'd been dead when he came back to life?'

Salvatore thought about it. 'No. I reckon he thought he'd been ill.'

'But how could he walk? Dead people's bodies are all hard. Remember how hard that cat we found was.'

'What cat?' He threw and hit the boiler again. His aim was infallible.

'The black cat, by the stream…do you remember?'

'Yes, I remember. Skull broke it in half.'

'If somebody's dead and they wake up, they don't walk right and they go crazy because their brain's rotted and they say weird things, don't you think?'

'I suppose so.'

'Do you reckon it's possible to bring a dead man back to life or do you think only Jesus Christ in person can do it?'

Salvatore scratched his head. 'I don't know. My aunt told me a true story. One day a man's son was run over by a car and he was killed and all mangled up. The father couldn't go on living, he felt ill, he cried all day, he went to a wizard and gave him all his money to bring his son back to life. The wizard said, "Go home and wait. Your son will return tonight." The father waited, but the son didn't come home, so in the end he went to bed. He was just falling asleep when he heard footsteps in the kitchen. He got up feeling very happy and saw his son, he was all mangled up and had one arm missing and his head was split open, with the brains running out and he said he hated him because he'd left him in the middle of the road to go with women and it was his fault he was dead.'

'So?'

'So the father got some petrol and set fire to him.'

'I don't blame him.' I threw and finally hit the target. 'Point! Four–two.'

Salvatore bent down to look for a stone. 'No, I don't blame him either.'

'But do you think it's a true story?'

'No.'

'Nor do I.'

I woke up because I needed a pee. My father had come back. I heard his voice in the kitchen.

There were visitors. They were quarrelling, interrupting each other, trading insults. Papa was very angry.

That evening we had gone to bed straight after supper.

I had fluttered around mama like a moth, to make it up. I had even peeled the potatoes, but she had been grouchy to me all afternoon. At supper she had banged down the plates in front of us and we had eaten in silence, while she bustled round the kitchen and looked at the road.

My sister was asleep. I knelt on the bed and looked out of the window.

The truck was parked beside a big dark car with a silver

front. A rich man's car.

I was dying for a pee, but to reach the bathroom I would have to go through the kitchen. With all those people I felt embarrassed, but I was practically wetting my pants.

I got up and went to the door. I grasped the handle. I counted. 'One, two, three…four, five, six.' And I gently opened it.

They were sitting at the table.

Italo Natale, Skull's father. Pietro Mura, the barber. Angela Mura. Felice. Papa. And an old man I had never seen before. He must be Sergio, papa's friend.

They were smoking. Their faces were red and tired and their eyes were bleary.

The table was covered with empty bottles, ashtrays full of cigarette stubs, packets of Nazionali and Milde Sorte, breadcrumbs. The fan was spinning, but it wasn't doing any good. The heat was suffocating. The television was on, without the volume. There was a smell of tomatoes, sweat and insecticide burners.

Mama was making the coffee.

I looked at the old man, who was taking a cigarette from a packet of Dunhill.

I later found out that his name was Sergio Materia. At the time he was seventy-seven, and he came from Rome, where he had achieved notoriety, twenty years earlier, as a result of a robbery at a fur shop on Monte Mario and a raid on the central branch of the Banca dell'Agricoltura. A week after the robbery he had bought a rosticceria-tavola calda in Piazza Bologna. He wanted to launder the money, but the carabinieri had busted him on opening day. He had done a long stretch in prison, had been released for good conduct and had emigrated to South America.

Sergio Materia was thin. With a bald head. Above his ears grew some sparse yellowish hair, which he tied back in a ponytail. He had a long nose and sunken eyes and his cheeks were dappled by at least two days' growth of white beard. His long blondish eyebrows looked like tufts of fur glued onto his forehead. His neck was wrinkled, and blotchy, as if it had been whitened with bleach. He was wearing a light-blue suit and a brown silk shirt. A pair of gold-rimmed glasses rested on his shiny scalp. And a golden chain with a sun pendant nestled among the hairs of his chest. On his wrist he wore a solid gold watch.

He was in a rage. 'Right from the start, you people have made one mistake after another.' He had a funny way of talking. 'And this guy's a moron.' He pointed at Felice. He looked at him the way you look at a dog turd. He picked up a toothpick and started cleaning his yellow teeth.

Felice was bent over the table drawing patterns on the tablecloth with his fork. He was the spitting image of his brother when he got told off by his mama.

The old man scratched his throat. 'I told them up North we couldn't rely on you. You're incompetent. It was a shitty idea. You've screwed up one thing after another. You play with fire.' He threw the toothpick in his plate. 'I'm a fool! I sit here wasting my time…If things had gone as they should have done I'd have been in Brazil by this time, and instead of that I'm stuck here in this lousy hole.'

Papa tried to argue. 'Sergio, listen…Don't worry…things aren't yet…'

But the old man shut him up. 'What fucking things? You'd better shut up, because you're worse than the others.

And you know why? Because you don't realise it. You're incompetent. All calm, sure of yourself, and you've fucked up one thing after another. You're an imbecile.'

Papa tried to answer, then he swallowed and lowered his gaze.

He had called him an imbecile.

I felt as if I'd been stabbed in the side. Nobody had ever talked to papa like that. Papa was the boss of Acqua Traverse. And that disgusting old man, who had appeared out of nowhere, was insulting him in front of everyone.

Why didn't papa throw him out?

Suddenly no one talked any more. They sat in silence, while the old man started picking his teeth again and looking at the lampshade.

The old man was like the emperor. When the emperor's in a black mood everyone has to keep quiet. Including papa.

'The news! Here's the news!' said Barbara's father fidgeting on his seat. 'It's starting!'

'Turn it up! Teresa, turn it up! And switch off the light,' papa said to mama.

At my house the light was always switched off when we watched television. It was compulsory. Mama rushed to the volume control and then to the light switch.

The room fell into half-light. Everyone turned towards the TV set. Like when Italy were playing.

Hidden behind the door, I saw them turn into dark silhouettes tinged with blue by the screen.

The newsreader was talking about a crash between two trains near Florence, some people had been killed, but nobody cared.

Mama was putting the sugar in the coffee. And they

were saying, 'One for me, two for me, none for me.'

Barbara's mother said, 'Maybe they won't mention it. They didn't yesterday. Maybe no one's interested any more.'

'Shut up, you!' the old man snapped.

It was the right moment to go and have my pee. All I had to do was reach my parents' bedroom. From there I could get into the bathroom and do it in the dark.

I imagined I was a black panther. I crawled out of the room on all fours. I was a few metres from safety when Skull's father got up from the sofa and came towards me.

I squashed down flat on the floor. Italo Natale fetched the cigarettes from the table and went back to sit on the sofa. I breathed a sigh and started moving forward. The door was within reach, I had made it, I had got there. I was starting to relax, when they all shouted at once: 'Here it is! Here it is! Quiet! Quiet everybody!'

I craned my neck over the sofa and nearly had a heart attack.

Behind the newsreader was a picture of the boy.

The boy in the hole.

He was blond. Well washed, his hair neatly combed, smartly dressed in a checked shirt, he was smiling and clutching an engine from an electric train set.

The newsreader went on, 'The search goes on for little Filippo Carducci, son of the Lombard businessman Giovanni Carducci, who was kidnapped two months ago in Pavia. The carabinieri and the investigating magistrates are following a new trail which is thought to lead…'

I didn't hear any more.

They were shouting. Papa and the old man jumped to their feet.

The boy's name was Filippo. Filippo Carducci.

'We are now broadcasting an appeal from Signora Luisa Carducci to the kidnappers, recorded this morning.'

'What's this cow want now?' said papa.

'Bitch! You fucking bitch!' growled Felice from the back. His father cuffed him round the head. 'Shut up!'

Barbara's mother seconded him. 'Silly idiot!'

'For Christ's sake! Will you all shut up!' shrieked the old man. 'I want to hear!'

A lady appeared. Elegant. Blonde. She was neither young nor old, but she was beautiful. She was sitting in a big leather armchair in a room full of books. Her eyes were glistening. She was squeezing her hands as if they might escape from her. She sniffed and said, looking us in the eyes, 'I'm Filippo Carducci's mother. I'm appealing to my son's kidnappers. Please don't hurt him. He's a good boy, polite and very shy. Please treat him well. I'm sure you know what love and understanding are. Even if you haven't got any children I'm sure you can imagine what it means when they're taken away from you. The ransom you've asked for is very high, but my husband and I are prepared to give you everything we own to have Filippo back with us. You've threatened to cut off one of his ears. I beg you, I implore you not to do it…'

She dried her eyes, got her breath back and went on. 'We're doing all we can. Please. God will reward you if you are merciful. Tell Filippo that his mama and papa haven't forgotten him and that they love him.'

Papa made the scissors sign with his fingers. '*Two* ears we'll cut off. *Two*.'

The old man added, 'Yeah, that'll teach you to talk on TV, you tramp!'

And they all started shouting again.

I slipped back into my bedroom, shut the door, climbed up on the windowsill and did it outside.

It had been papa and the others who taken the boy away from that lady on television.

The pee drummed on the tarpaulin of the truck and the droplets shone in the light of the streetlamp.

'Be careful, Michele, you mustn't go out at night,' mama always said. 'When it's dark the bogeyman comes out and takes the children away and sells them to the gypsies.'

Papa was the bogeyman.

By day he was good, but at night he was bad.

All the others were gypsies. Gypsies disguised as people. And that old man was the king of the gypsies and papa was his servant. Mama wasn't, though.

I had imagined the gypsies as elf-like creatures that moved very quickly, with foxes' ears and chickens' feet. But they were really just ordinary people.

Why didn't they give him back to her? What use was a barmy little boy to them? Filippo's mother was distressed, you could see that. If she asked on television it meant she cared a lot about her son.

And papa wanted to cut off his ears.

'What are you doing?' I jumped, turned round and nearly peed on the bed.

Maria had woken up.

I put my dick back in my pants.

'Nothing.'

'You were peeing, I saw you.'

'I couldn't wait.'

'What's going on in there?'

If I told Maria that papa was the bogeyman she might go out of her mind. I shrugged.

'Nothing.'

'What are they arguing about?'

'Nothing special.'

'But what?'

I said the first thing that came into my head. 'They're playing bingo.'

'Bingo?'

'Yes. They're arguing about who draws the numbers.'

'Who's winning?'

'Sergio, papa's friend.'

'Has he arrived?'

'Yes.'

'What's he like?'

'Old. Go to sleep now.'

'I can't. It's too hot. It's noisy. When are they going?'

In the other room they were still shouting.

I got down from the window. 'I don't know.'

'Michele, will you tell me a bedtime story so I can go to sleep?'

Papa told us stories about Agnolotto in Africa. Agnolotto was a little town dog who hid in a suitcase and ended up in Africa by mistake, among the lions and elephants. We liked that story a lot. Agnolotto could stand up to the jackals. And he had a marmot friend. When papa came home he usually told us a new episode.

It was the first time Maria had ever asked me to tell her a bedtime story, I felt very honoured. The trouble was I didn't know the stories. 'Well, I would, but…I don't know any,' I had to admit.

'Yes you do. You do know some.'

'Which ones do I know?'

'Do you remember the story Barbara's mother told us that time? The one about Pierino Pierone?'

'Oh yes!'

'Will you tell it to me?'

'Okay, but I can't remember all of it.'

'Will you tell it to me in the tent?'

'All right.' That way at least we wouldn't hear the screams in the kitchen. I got into my sister's bed and we pulled the sheet over our heads.

'Begin,' she whispered in my ear.

'Well, there was a boy called Pierino Pierone who always climbed up on the trees to eat the fruit. One day he was up there when the Wicked Witch arrived. And she said, "Pierino Pierone, give me a pear, I'm terribly hungry." And Pierino Pierone threw her a pear.'

Maria interrupted me. 'You haven't told me what the Wicked Witch looks like.'

'Quite right. She's very ugly. She's got no hair on the top of her head. She's got a ponytail and a long nose. She's tall and she eats children. And her husband's the bogeyman…'

While I told the story, I could see papa cutting off Filippo's ears and putting them in his pocket. And fixing them to the rear-view mirror of the truck, as he had that furry tail.

'That's not true. She's not married. Tell it properly. I know the story.'

'Pierino Pierone threw her a pear and it landed in the cow shit.'

Maria started chuckling. She was very fond of things with doo-doo in them.

'The Wicked Witch said again, "Pierino Pierone, give me a pear, I'm terribly hungry." "Catch this!" And he threw her a pear into the cow piss. And made it all dirty.'

More chuckles.

'The witch asked him again. And he threw another pear into the cow sick.'

She prodded me with her elbow. 'That's not in it. It's not fair. Don't be silly.'

With my sister you couldn't change the story the slightest little bit. 'Then...'

What were they doing in the other room? It sounded as if someone had broken a plate. 'Then Pierino Pierone got down from the tree and gave her a pear. The Wicked Witch caught him and tied him up in a sack and put him over her shoulder. Since Pierino Pierone ate peppers, which are very heavy, the witch couldn't carry him and had to stop every five minutes and after a while she had to have a pee, so she put down the sack and hid behind a tree. Pierino Pierone cut the rope with his teeth and got out and put a little wash-bear inside...'

'A little wash-bear?'

I had said it on purpose, to see if Maria knew about them.

'Yes, a little wash-bear.'

'Who are they?'

'They're little bears and if you leave your clothes near the river they come and wash them for you.'

'Where do they live?'

'In the North.'

'And then?' Maria knew it was a stone Pierino Pierone had put in the sack, but she didn't say anything.

'The Wicked Witch picked up the sack again and put it on her back and when she got home she said to her daughter, "Margherita Margheritone, come down and open the door and get the big pot ready to boil Pierino Pierone." Margherita Margheritone put the pot of water on the fire and the Wicked Witch emptied the sack into it and the little wash-bear jumped out and started biting both of them, went down into the yard and started eating the hens, and threw all the rubbish in the air. The witch grew very angry and went out again to look for Pierino Pierone. She found him and put him in the sack and didn't stop anywhere. When she got home she said to Margherita Margheritone, "Take him down and lock him in the cellar, tomorrow we'll have him for dinner…"'

I stopped.

Maria was asleep and that was a nasty story.

I FOUND the old man in the bathroom next morning.

I opened the door and there he was shaving, bent over the washbasin, with his face up against the mirror and a cigarette hanging from his lips. He wore a threadbare vest and some yellowed long johns from which two slender, hairless stilts emerged. On his feet he had black half-boots with the zips down.

He had a pungent smell, hidden by the talc and after-shave.

He turned towards me and looked me up and down with puffy eyes, one cheek covered with foam and the razor in his hand. 'Who are you?'

I pointed a finger at my chest. 'Me?'

'Yes, you.'

'Michele…Michele Amitrano.'

'I'm Sergio. Pleased to meet you.'

I stretched out my hand. 'How do you do.' That's how they had taught me to reply at school.

The old man rinsed the razor in the water. 'Don't you

know you're supposed to knock before going into the bathroom? Didn't your parents teach you that?'

'I'm sorry.' I wanted to leave but I stood rooted to the spot. Like when you see a cripple and you try not to look at him but you can't help it.

He started shaving his neck. 'Are you Pino's son?'

'Yes.'

He scrutinised me in the mirror. 'Are you a quiet child?'

'Yes.'

'I like quiet children. Good boy. You don't take after your father, then. And are you obedient?'

'Yes.'

'Then go out and shut the door.'

I ran to find mama. She was in my room taking the sheets off Maria's bed. I tugged at her dress. 'Mama! Mama, who's that old man in the bathroom?'

'Let go of me, Michele, I'm busy. That's Sergio, your father's friend. He told you he was coming. He'll be staying with us for a few days.'

'Why?'

She lifted up the mattress and turned it over. 'Because that's what your father's decided.'

'And where's he going to sleep?'

'In your sister's bed.'

'What about her?'

'She'll sleep with us.'

'And where do I sleep?'

'In your bed.'

'You mean the old man's to sleep in the bedroom with me?'

Mama took a deep breath. 'Yes.'

'In the night?'

'Well, when do you think? In the daytime?'

'Can't Maria sleep with him? And I'll sleep with you.'

'Don't be silly.' She started putting on the clean sheets. 'Go outside, I'm busy.'

I threw myself on the ground and clung to her ankles. 'Mama, please, I don't want to sleep with that man. Please, I want to be with you. In the bed with you.'

She breathed hard. 'There's not enough room. You're too big.'

'Mama, please. I'll curl up in the corner. I'll make myself really small.'

'I said no.'

'Please,' I implored her. 'Please. I'll be good. You'll see.'

'Stop it.' She stood me up and looked me in the eyes. 'Michele, I just don't know what to do with you. Why do you never do as you're told? I can't stand it any more. We've got so many problems and now *you* start. You don't understand. Please...'

I shook my head. 'I don't want to. I don't want to sleep with that man. I'm not going to.'

She took the pillowcase off the pillow. 'That's how things are. If you don't like it, tell your father.'

'But he'll take me away...'

Mama stopped making the bed and turned. 'What did you say? Say that again.'

I whispered. 'He'll take me away...'

She peered at me with her black eyes. 'What do you mean?'

'You want him to take me away...You hate me. You're

nasty. You and papa hate me. I know you do.'

'Who tells you such things?' She grabbed me by the arm but I wriggled free and fled.

I was running downstairs and I could hear her calling me. 'Michele! Michele! Come back here!'

'I'm not sleeping with him. No, I'm not sleeping with that man.'

I ran off to the stream and climbed up the carob.

I would never sleep with that old man. He had taken Filippo. And as soon as I went to sleep he would take me too. He would put me in a sack and whisk me off.

And then he would cut off my ears.

Was it possible to live without ears? Wouldn't you die? I was very attached to my ears. Papa and the old man must have already cut Filippo's off. While I was up in my tree, he, in his hole, was earless.

I wondered if they had bandaged up his head?

I must go. And I must tell him about his mother, that she still loved him and that she had said so on television, so everybody knew it.

But I was scared. What if I found papa and the old man at the house?

I looked at the horizon. The sky was flat and grey and weighed down on the fields of wheat. The hill was over there, gigantic, veiled by the heat.

If I'm careful they won't see me, I said to myself.

'O partisan, take me away, for they have to bury me. O partisan, take me away. *O bella ciao ciao ciao.*' I heard a voice singing.

I looked down. Barbara Mura was dragging Togo along, she had tied some string round his neck and was pulling him towards the water. 'Now mama's going to give you a little bath. You'll be all clean. Are you pleased? Of course you're pleased.' But Togo didn't look pleased. Rump on the ground, he was digging in his paws and shaking his head, trying to get free of the noose. 'You'll look lovely. And I'll take you to Lucignano. We'll go and have an ice-cream and I'll buy you a lead.' She grabbed him, kissed him, slipped off her sandals, took a couple of steps into the bog and ducked him in that stinking slime.

Togo squirmed but Barbara held him fast by his scruff and his collar. She pushed him under. I saw him disappear in the mud.

She started singing again. 'One fine morning I woke early. *O bella ciao! Bella ciao! Bella ciao ciao ciao!*'

She didn't pull him out again.

She wanted to kill him.

I shouted. 'What are you doing? Let him go!'

Barbara gave a start and nearly fell in the water. She released the dog, who resurfaced and struggled to the bank.

With one jump I got down from the tree.

'What are you doing here?' Barbara asked me testily.

'What were you doing?'

'Nothing. I was washing him.'

'No you weren't. You wanted to kill him.'

'No I didn't.'

'Swear it!'

'I swear by God and all the saints!' she put her hand on her heart. 'He's crawling with ticks and fleas. That's why I was giving him a bath.'

I didn't know whether to believe her or not.

She grabbed Togo, who was standing on a stone and wagging his tail happily. He had already forgotten his nasty experience. 'See for yourself if I'm telling the truth.' She lifted one of his ears.

'Oh my God, ugh!'

All around and inside the earhole was teeming with ticks. It was revolting. With those little heads of theirs buried in the skin, with their little black legs and their dark-brown stomachs, swollen and round like little chocolate eggs.

'See? They're sucking his blood.'

I twisted my nose doubtfully. 'And will the mud get rid of them?'

'On television Tarzan said elephants take mud baths to get the insects off.'

'But Togo isn't an elephant.'

'So what? He's still an animal.'

'I reckon you have to pull them off,' I said. 'The mud won't get rid of them.'

'But how?'

'With your hands.'

'Who wants to do that? It gives me the creeps.'

'I'll try.' With two fingers I gripped a big bloated one, shut my eyes and pulled hard. Togo whimpered, but the monster came away. I put it on a stone and we inspected it. It was wiggling its legs but couldn't move though, it was swollen with blood.

'Die, vampire! Die!' Barbara squashed it with a stone, turning it into a red mush.

I must have pulled off at least twenty. Barbara held the dog still for me. After a while I got fed up. Togo couldn't stand any more either. He yelped as soon as I touched him. 'We'll get the others off another day. All right?'

'All right.' Barbara looked around. 'I'm going. What are you going to do?'

'I'm going to stay here a bit longer.' As soon as she left I would get the Crock and go and see Filippo.

She put the string round Togo's neck again.

'See you later then?' she said as she went off.

'Yes.'

She stopped. 'There's a man at your house. With that grey car. Is he a relative of yours?'

'No he isn't.'

'He came round to my house today too.'

'What did he want?'

'I don't know. He was talking to papa. Then they went off. I think your papa was there too. In the big car.'

Of course. They were going to cut off Filippo's ears.

She grimaced and asked me, 'Do you like that man?'

'No I don't.'

'Nor do I.'

She stood there in silence. She didn't seem to want to go any more. She turned and whispered thanks.

'What for?'

'The other day…When you did the forfeit instead of me.'

I shrugged. 'That's all right.'

'Listen…' She went all red. She looked at me for a second and said, 'Would you like to be my boyfriend?'

My face was suddenly boiling. 'What?'

She bent down to stroke Togo. 'My boyfriend.'

'You mean, you and me?'

'Yes.'

I lowered my head and looked at my toes. 'Well…not really.'

She let out a suppressed sigh. 'Never mind. We're not even the same age.' She ran her fingers through her hair. 'Bye, then.'

'Bye.'

She went off pulling Togo along behind her.

I became scared of vipers, just like that, quite suddenly.

Until that day, when I went up the hill, I had never thought about vipers.

I kept having visions of that hound that had been bitten on the nose by a viper in April. The poor beast was lying in a corner of the shed, panting, with glazed eyes, white foam on his gums and his tongue hanging out.

'There's nothing more we can do for him,' Skull's father had said. 'The poison's got into his heart.'

We all stood round looking at him.

'Let's take him to Lucignano. To the vet,' I had suggested.

'Waste of money. The guy's a crook, he'd squirt a syringeful of water into him and give you the dog back dead. Just go away, let him die in peace.' He had pushed us outside. Maria had started crying.

I was going through the wheat and I seemed to see snakes slithering about everywhere. I hopped like a quail and whacked a stick on the ground, scattering the crickets and grasshoppers. The sun beat down on my head and neck, there wasn't a breath of wind and in the distance the plain was all blurred.

By the time I reached the edge of the valley I was exhausted. A bit of shade and a drink of water was what I needed. I went into the wood.

But there was something different from usual. I stopped.

Under the birds, crickets and cicadas you could hear the sound of music.

I dived behind a tree trunk.

I couldn't see anything from there, but the music seemed to be coming from the house.

I should have got out of there fast, but curiosity drove me to take a look. If I was careful, if I stayed among the trees, I wouldn't be seen. Hiding among the oaks I moved in closer to the clearing.

The music was louder. It was a well-known song. I had heard it dozens of times. It was sung by a blonde lady with a smartly dressed gentleman. I had seen them on television. I liked that song.

There was a boulder covered with green tufts of moss right at the edge of the clearing, a good shelter, I crawled up behind it.

I craned my neck and peered over.

Parked in front of the house was Felice's 127, with the doors and the boot open. The music came from the car radio. It wasn't very clear, it crackled.

Felice came out of the cowshed. He was in his underpants. He had army boots on his feet and the usual black bandanna round his neck. He was dancing with arms outspread, grinding like a belly dancer.

'You never change, you never change, you never change…' He sang in falsetto, with the radio.

Then he stopped and went on in a deep voice.

'You are my yesterday, my today. My always. Anxiety.'

And in the woman's voice: 'Now, at last, you can try. Call me tormentress, sigh. While you're about it.'

He pointed at someone. 'You're like the wind that brings the violins and the roses.'

'Words, words, words…'

'Listen to me.'

'Words, words, words…'

'I implore you.'

He was very good. He did it all on his own. Male and female. And when he was the man he acted tough. Narrowed eyes and barely parted lips.

'Words, words, words…'

'I swear to you.'

Then he threw himself on the ground, in the dust, and started doing press-ups. Two-handed, one-handed, with clap, and he went on singing, jerkily.

'Word, words, words, words, words, only words, words, between us.'

I left.

In Acqua Traverse they were playing one-two-three-star.

Skull, Barbara and Remo were standing still, under the sun, in strange positions.

Salvatore, with his head against the wall, shouted. 'One, two, three, staaaaar!' He turned and saw Skull.

Skull always overdid it, instead of going three steps he went fifteen and got caught. Then he wouldn't take it. You would tell him you had seen him, but he wouldn't listen to you. In his eyes everybody else cheated. Not him, he was a saint. And if you said anything he would start shoving you. One way or another he always won. Even with dolls he would have found a way of winning.

I passed between the houses, pedalling slowly. I was tired and angry. I hadn't managed to tell Filippo about his mother.

Papa's truck was parked outside the house, next to the old man's big grey car.

I was hungry. I had run off without having breakfast. But I wasn't too keen on going indoors.

Skull came over to me. 'Where did you get to?'

'I went for a ride.'

'You're always going off on your own. Where do you go?' He didn't like it when you minded your own business.

'To the stream.'

He eyed me suspiciously. 'What do you do there?'

I shrugged. 'Nothing much. Climb the tree.'

He made the disgusted face of someone who's just eaten a rotten apple.

Togo arrived and started biting the wheel of my bike.

Skull aimed a kick at him. 'Get lost, you mutt. He punctures tyres with those fucking teeth of his.'

Togo fled to Barbara, who was sitting on the wall, and jumped into her lap. Barbara called hello to me. I waved back.

Skull observed the scene. 'What's this, have you made friends with fatso?'

'No…'

He peered at me to see if I was telling the truth.

'No, I swear I haven't!'

He relaxed. 'Oh, I see. Fancy a game of soccer?'

I didn't, but saying no to him was dangerous. 'Isn't it a bit hot?'

He grabbed my handlebars. 'You're being a bit of a shit, you know that?'

I was scared. 'Why?' Skull could suddenly flip and decide to pull you off your bike and beat you up.

'Because you are.'

Luckily Salvatore appeared. He was bouncing the ball on his head. Then he trapped it with his foot and tucked it under his arm. 'Hi, Michele.'

'Hi.'

Skull asked him, 'Fancy a game?'

'No.'

Skull lost his temper. 'You're pieces of shit, both of you! Right, you know what I'm doing? I'm going to Lucignano.' And he stomped off in a filthy mood.

We had a good laugh, then Salvatore said to me, 'I'm going home. Do you want to come with me and play Subbuteo?'

'I don't really feel like it.'

He gave me a pat on the back. 'All right. See you later then. Bye.' He went off juggling with the ball.

I liked Salvatore. I liked the way he always kept calm and didn't fly off the handle every five minutes. With Skull you had to think three times before you said anything.

I cycled over to the drinking fountain.

Maria had taken the enamelled bowl and was using it as a swimming pool for her Barbies.

She had two—one normal, the other all blackened with one arm melted and no hair.

That was my fault. One evening I had seen the story of Joan of Arc on television and I had picked up the Barbie doll and thrown her in the fire shouting 'Burn! Witch! Burn!' When I had recognised she really was burning, I had grabbed her by one foot and thrown her in the saucepan where the minestrone was cooking.

Mama had taken away my bike for a week and made me eat all the minestrone by myself. Maria had begged her to buy her another doll. 'I'll get you one for your birthday. Play with this one for now. Blame that stupid brother of yours.' And Maria had made the best of it. The beautiful Barbie was called Paola and the burnt one Poor Poppet.

'Hi, Maria,' I said getting off my bike.

She put one hand over her forehead to shield her eyes from the sun. 'Papa's been looking for you…Mama's cross.'

'I know.'

She took Poor Poppet and put her in the swimming pool. 'You're always making her cross.'

'I'm going upstairs.'

'Papa said he's got to talk to Sergio and he doesn't want us around.'

'But I'm hungry…'

She took an apricot out of her trouser pocket. 'Do you want this?'

'Yes.' It was warm and squashy, but I gulped it down and spat the stone into the distance.

Papa came out onto the balcony, saw me and called to me. 'Michele, come here.' He was wearing a shirt and shorts.

I didn't want to talk to him. 'I can't, I'm busy!'

He beckoned me up. 'Come here.'

I leaned my bike against the wall and went up the steps hanging my head resignedly.

Papa sat down on the top step. 'Come and sit here, next to me.' He pulled a packet of Nazionali out of his shirt pocket, took a cigarette, put it in the holder and lit it.

'You and I have got to talk.'

He didn't seem all that angry.

We sat there in silence. Looking over the roofs at the yellow fields.

'Hot, isn't it?'

'Very.'

He blew out a cloud of smoke. 'Where do you get to all day long, for goodness' sake?'

'Nowhere.'

'Yes you do. You must go somewhere.'

'Riding around here.'

'On your own?'

'Yes.'

'What's the matter? Don't you like being with your friends?'

'Yes, I do. It's just that I like being on my own too.'

He nodded, his eyes lost in the void. I glanced at him. He seemed older, his black hair was speckled with a few white strands, his cheeks had sunk and he looked as if he hadn't slept for a week.

'You've upset your mother.'

I broke off a twig of rosemary from a pot and started fiddling with it. 'I didn't mean to.'

'She said you don't want to sleep with Sergio.'

'Well, I don't…'

'Why?'

'Because I want to sleep with you and mama. In your bed. All together. If we squeeze up, we'll all fit in.'

'What's Sergio going to think if you don't sleep with him?'

'I don't care what he thinks.'

'That's no way to treat guests. Suppose you went to stay with someone and nobody wanted to sleep with you. What would you think?'

'I wouldn't care, I'd like a room all to myself. Like in a hotel.'

He smiled faintly and with two fingers threw the dog-end into the street.

I asked him, 'Is Sergio your boss? Is that why he's got to stay with us?'

He looked at me in surprise. 'What do you mean is he my boss?'

'I mean does he decide things?'

'No, he doesn't decide anything. He's a friend of mine.'

It wasn't true. The old man wasn't his friend, he was his boss. I knew that. He could even call him names.

'Papa, where do you sleep when you go to the North?'

'Why?'

'I just wondered.'

'In a hotel, or wherever I can, in the truck sometimes.'

'But what happens at night in the North?'

He looked at me, breathed in through his nose and asked me, 'What's up? Aren't you pleased I've come home?'

'Yes.'

'Tell me the truth.'

'Yes, I am pleased.'

He squeezed me in his arms, tightly. I could smell his

sweat. He whispered in my ear. 'Hug me, Michele, hug me! Let me feel how strong you are.'

I hugged him as hard as I could and I couldn't help crying. The tears ran down my face and my throat tightened.

'Hey, are you crying?'

I sobbed. 'No, I'm not crying.'

He took a crumpled handkerchief out of his pocket. 'Dry away those tears, if anybody sees you they'll think you're a sissy. Michele, I'm very busy at the moment so you must do as you're told. Your mother's tired. Stop all this nonsense. If you're good, as soon as I've finished I'll take you to the seaside. We'll go on a pedalo.'

I wheezed. 'What's a pedalo?'

'It's a boat that has pedals like a bike instead of oars.'

I dried my tears. 'Can you get to Africa in one?'

'It'd take a lot of pedalling to get to Africa.'

'I want to go away from Acqua Traverse.'

'Why, don't you like it any more?'

I gave him back his handkerchief. 'Let's go to the North.'

'What do you want to go away for?'

'I don't know…I don't like being here any more.'

He looked into the distance. 'We'll go there.'

I broke off another twig of rosemary. It had a nice smell. 'Do you know about the little wash-bears?'

He frowned. 'The little wash-bears?'

'Yes.'

'No, what are they?'

'They're bears that do the washing…But maybe they don't exist.'

Papa got up and stretched his back. 'Aahh! Listen, I'm

going indoors, I've got to talk to Sergio. Why don't you run off and play? It'll be suppertime soon.' He opened the door and was about to go in, but he stopped. 'Mama's made tagliatelle. Afterwards, say sorry to her.'

At that moment Felice arrived. He braked his 127 in a cloud of dust and got out as if there was a swarm of wasps inside.

'Felice!' papa shouted. 'Come up a minute.'

Felice nodded and as he passed me he cuffed me on the back of the head and said, 'How're you doing, little sap?'

Now there was nobody with Filippo.

The bucket of shit was full. The saucepan of water empty.

Filippo kept his head wrapped up in the blanket. He hadn't even noticed I had come down into the hole.

His ankle looked worse to me, it was more swollen and purple. The flies were homing in on it.

I moved closer. 'Hey!' He gave no sign of having heard me. 'Hey! Can you hear me?' I moved even closer. 'Can you hear me?'

He sighed. 'Yes.'

Papa hadn't cut off his ears, then.

'Your name's Filippo, isn't it?'

'Yes.'

I had been rehearsing on the way. 'I've come to tell you something very important. Um…Your mother says she loves you. And she says she misses you. She said so yesterday on television. On the news. She said you mustn't worry… and that she doesn't want just your ears, she wants all of you.'

108

Nothing.

'Did you hear me?'

Nothing.

I repeated. 'Um…your mother says she loves you. And she says she misses you. She said so yesterday on television. She said you mustn't worry…and that she doesn't want just your ears.'

'My mother's dead.'

'What do you mean she's dead?'

From under the blanket he replied, 'My mother's dead.'

'What are you talking about? She's alive. I saw her myself, on television…'

'No she isn't, she's dead.'

I put my hand on my heart. 'I swear to you on the head of my sister Maria that she's alive. I saw her last night, she was on television. She was well. She's blonde. She's thin. She's a bit old…She's beautiful, though. She was sitting on a high, brown armchair. A big one. Like the ones kings have. And behind it there was a picture of a ship. Isn't that right?'

'Yes. The picture of the ship…' He spoke quietly, the words were muffled by the cloth.

'And you've got an electric train. With an engine and a funnel. I saw it.'

'I haven't got that any more. It got broken. Nanny threw it away.'

'Nanny? Who's nanny?'

'Liliana. She's dead too. And Peppino's dead. And papa's dead. And grandmother Arianna's dead. And my brother's dead. They're all dead. They're all dead and they live in holes like this one. And I'm in one too. Everybody. The

109

world's a place full of holes with dead people in them. And the moon's a ball all full of holes too and inside them there are other dead people.'

'No it isn't.' I put my hand on his back. 'There aren't any holes on it. The moon's normal. And your mother's not dead. I saw her. You must listen to me.'

He was silent for a while, then he asked me, 'Why doesn't she come here, then?'

I shook my head. 'I don't know.'

'Why doesn't she come and fetch me?'

'I don't know.'

'And why am I here?'

'I don't know.' Then I said, so quietly that he couldn't hear me. 'My father put you here.'

He gave me a kick. 'You don't know anything. Leave me alone. You're not the guardian angel. You're bad. Go away.' And he started crying.

I didn't know what to do. 'I'm not bad. It's nothing to do with me. Don't cry, please.'

He kept kicking. 'Go away. Go away.'

'Listen to me…'

'Go away!'

I sprang to my feet. 'I came out here for your sake, I rode all that way, twice, and you kick me out. All right, I'll go, but if I go I'm not coming back. Ever again. You'll stay here, on your own, for ever and they'll cut both your ears off.' I seized the rope and started to climb back up. I heard him crying. He sounded as if he was suffocating.

I got out of the hole and said to him, 'And I'm not your guardian angel!'

'Wait…'

'What do you want?'

'Stay…'

'No. You told me to go away and now I'm going.'

'Please. Stay with me.'

'No!'

'Please. Just for five minutes.'

'All right. Five minutes. But if you act crazy I'm going.'

'I won't.'

I went down. He touched my foot.

'Why don't you come out of that blanket?' I asked him and crouched down beside him.

'I can't, I'm blind…'

'What do you mean you're blind?'

'My eyes won't open. I want to open them but they stay closed. In the dark I can see. In the dark I'm not blind.' He hesitated. 'Do you know something, they told me you'd come back.'

'Who did?'

'The little wash-bears.'

'Stop going on about little wash-bears! Papa told me they don't exist. Are you thirsty?'

'Yes.'

I opened my bag and got out the bottle. 'Here you are.'

'Come here.' He lifted the blanket.

I made a face. 'Under there?' The idea rather gave me the creeps. But at least I would be able to see if he still had both his ears in place.

He started touching me. 'How old are you?' He ran his hands over my nose, my mouth, my eyes.

I was paralysed. 'Nine. What about you?'

'Nine.'

'When's your birthday?'

'The twelfth of September. And yours?'

'The twentieth of November.'

'What's your name?'

'Michele. Michele Amitrano. What year are you in at school?'

'The fourth. What about you?'

'The fourth.'

'Same.'

'Same.'

'I'm thirsty.'

I gave him the bottle.

He drank. 'That's good. Do you want some?'

I drank too. 'Can I lift the blanket a bit?' The heat and smell were stifling me.

'Only a bit though.'

I pulled it away just far enough to get some air and look at his face.

It was black. Filthy. His fine blond hair had mingled with the earth to form a hard dry mat. Clotted blood had sealed up his eyelids. His lips were black and split. His nostrils were blocked up with snot and scabs.

'Can I wash your face?' I asked him.

He craned his neck and raised his head and a smile opened on his battered lips. All his teeth had gone black.

I took off my T-shirt, moistened it with the water and started to clean his face.

Where I washed, the skin came white, so white it seemed transparent, like the flesh of a boiled fish. First on the forehead, then on the cheeks.

When I bathed his eyes he said: 'Careful, it hurts.'

'I'll be careful.'

I couldn't loosen the scabs. They were hard and thick. But I knew they were like the scabs dogs get. When you take them off, dogs can see again. I kept bathing them, softening them, till one eyelid rose and immediately shut again. Just an instant, enough for a ray of light to strike his eye.

'Aaaahhhaaa!' he shouted and stuck his head under the blanket like an ostrich.

I shook him. 'See? See? You're not blind! You're not blind at all!'

'I can't keep them open.'

'That's because you're always in the dark. But you can see, can't you?'

'Yes! You're small.'

'I'm not small. I'm nine years old.'

'You've got black hair.'

'That's right.'

It was very late. I would have to go home. 'But now I've got to go. I'll be back tomorrow.'

With his head under the blanket he said: 'Promise?'

'Promise.'

When the old man came into my room I was just getting organised to foil the monsters.

When I was small I always dreamed about monsters. And even now, as an adult, I sometimes dream about them, but I can't foil them any more.

They would just be waiting for me to fall asleep so they could frighten me.

Till, one night, I invented a way of not having nightmares.

I found a place where I could lock those misshapen terrifying creatures up and sleep serenely.

I would relax and wait for my eyelids to get heavy, and when I was on the point of dropping off, just at that precise moment, I would imagine I could see them walking, all together, up a slope. Like in the procession of the Madonna at Lucignano.

The Wicked Witch, hunchbacked and wrinkled. The four-legged werewolf with his torn clothes and white fangs. The bogeyman, a shadow who slithered like a snake among the stones. Lazarus, a corpse-eater, devoured by insects and enveloped in a cloud of flies. The ogre, a giant with small eyes and the goitre, great big shoes and a sack full of children on his back. The gypsies, fox-like creatures that walked on hens' feet. The man with the circle, a guy with an electric-blue tracksuit and a circle of light that he could throw a long, long way. The fish-man, who lived in the depths of the sea and carried his mother on his shoulders. The octopus boy, who was born with tentacles instead of legs and arms.

They all advanced together. Towards some indeterminate point. They were terrifying. And indeed nobody stopped to look at them.

Suddenly a bus appeared, it was all golden, with bells and little coloured lights. On its roof was a megaphone that blared out, 'Ladies and gentlemen, come aboard this bus of desires! Come aboard this magnificent bus, it'll take you all to the circus and you won't have to pay a lira! Free trips to the circus today! All aboard! All aboard!'

The monsters, delighted at this unexpected opportunity, got on the bus. At this point I imagined that my stomach opened up, a long cut gaped apart and they all walked happily into it.

Those suckers thought it was the circus. I closed up the wound and I'd got them. Now all I had to do was go to sleep with my hands on my stomach and I wouldn't have any nightmares.

I had just got them trapped when the old man came in, I lost concentration, took my hands away and they escaped. I shut my eyes and pretended to be asleep.

The old man made a lot of noises. He rummaged in his suitcase. He coughed. He puffed.

I covered my head with one arm and watched what he was doing.

A ray of light lit up one segment of the room. The old man was sitting on Maria's bed. Thin, hunched and dark. He was smoking. And when he inhaled I saw the beaky nose and sunken eyes become tinged with red. I could smell the smoke and the cologne. Now and then he shook his head. Then he snorted as if he was arguing with someone.

He started to get undressed. He took off his half-boots, his socks, his trousers, his shirt. He was left in his underpants. He had flaccid skin that hung from those long bones as if it had been sewn on to them. He threw his cigarette out of the window. The stub disappeared into the night like a burning fragment of volcanic rock. He untied his hair and he looked like an old, sick Tarzan. He lay down on the bed.

Now I couldn't see him any more, but he was near. Less than half a metre from my feet. If he stretched out his arm he could grab my ankle. I curled up like a hedgehog.

I mustn't sleep. If I fell asleep he might take me away.

I must think of something. Put nails in my bed. That would stop me sleeping.

He hawked. 'It's stifling in here. How can you stand it?'

I stopped breathing.

'I know you're not asleep.'

He wanted to get me.

'Crafty little devil, you are…Don't like me, do you?'

No, I don't like you! I wanted to reply. But I couldn't. I was asleep. And even if I'd been awake I would never have dared to say it.

'My kids didn't like me either.' He picked up from the floor a bottle mama had put there for him and took a couple of swigs. 'Warm as piss,' he grumbled. 'Two, I had. One's alive, but he might as well be dead. The other's dead, but he might as well be alive. The one who's alive's called Giuliano. He's older than you. Doesn't live in Italy any more. Went abroad. To India…five years ago. Lives in a community. They've filled his head with crap. He's shaved his head. Wears orange clothes and thinks he's an Indian himself. And thinks we have lots of lives. Dopes himself like a dog and he'll die like a dog out there. I'm certainly not going out there to bring him back…'

He had a fit of coughing. Dry. Lung-bursting. He got his breath back and went on. 'Francesco died five years ago. Would have been thirty-two next October. Now he was a good boy, I loved him.' He lit another cigarette. 'One day he met a girl. I saw her and didn't like her. Right from the start. Said she was a gym teacher. Little tart…skinny blonde…half Slav. The Slavs are the worst. Wrapped him up like a toffee, she did. She was down on her luck and she saw Francesco and she latched on to him because

Francesco's a good boy, generous, always getting taken for a ride by everyone. God knows what she did to get him eating out of her hand like that. Afterwards I heard the bitch was in cahoots with some kind of magician. A piece of shit who must have put a spell on him. The two of them together fucked him up. Sapped his strength. He'd grown as thin as a rake. Big strong lad he was, turned into a skeleton, could hardly stand upright. One day he comes along and says he's getting married. Wouldn't listen to reason. I tried to tell him she'd ruin him, but what can you do, it was his life. They got married. Went off on honeymoon by car. Heading for Positano and Amalfi, on the coast. Two days go by and he doesn't call. That's normal, I say to myself, they're on honeymoon. He'll call. And who does call? The Sorrento police. They say I've got to go there at once. I ask why. Can't tell me over the phone. I've got to go there if I want to find out. They say it's about my son. How the fuck could I go? There was no way I could. If they checked up on me I was in the shit. I was on the wanted list because I'd skipped parole. They'd slam me straight back inside. So I got a guy I know to ring them. Guy with a bit of pull. And he tells me my son's dead. What do you mean dead? He tells me he killed himself, threw himself off a cliff. Fell two hundred metres and smashed onto the rocks. My son? Francesco kill himself? Who were they trying to kid? I couldn't go. So I sent that fool of a mother of his to see what had happened.'

'What had happened?' I blurted out.

'They said Francesco stopped along the road to look at the view, she stayed in the car, he took a picture of her, then climbed up on the wall and jumped off. A guy takes a

117

picture of his wife and then jumps off a cliff? He says they found him lying with his dick sticking out of his trousers and his camera round his neck. You reckon a guy who wants to kill himself takes a photograph, pulls out his dick and then jumps off a cliff? Bullshit! I know what really happened…Admire the view, my arse! Francesco stopped because he needed a piss. He didn't want to do it in the middle of the road. He's a well-bred young man. He climbed on the wall and relieved himself and that tart pushed him off. But nobody believes me. One shove and he's gone. Murdered.'

'But why?'

'Good question. Why? I don't know. He didn't have a lira. I just don't know. I can't sleep at nights. But that bitch paid for it…I gave her…Well, never mind that, it's late. Good night.'

He threw the cigarette out of the window and lay down to sleep and in two minutes he was asleep and in three he was snoring.

WHEN I woke up the old man had gone. He had left the
bed unmade, a packet of Dunhill crumpled up on the
windowsill, his underpants on the floor and the bottle of
water half-empty.

It was warm. The cicadas were singing.

I got up and looked into the kitchen. Mama was ironing
and listening to the radio. My sister was playing on the
floor. I shut the door.

The old man's suitcase was under the bed. I opened it
and looked inside.

Clothes. A bottle of perfume. A flask of Stock 84. A
carton of cigarette packets. A folder with a little pack of
photographs in it. The first was of a tall thin boy, dressed
in blue mechanic's overalls. He was smiling. He looked like
the old man. Francesco, the boy who had jumped off the
cliff with his pecker out.

There were some newspaper cuttings in the folder too.
Articles about Francesco's death. There was a picture of
his wife too. She looked like a television dancer. I also found

a lined school exercise book with a coloured plastic cover. I opened it. Written on the first page was: This exercise book belongs to Filippo Carducci. Fourth C.

The first few pages had been torn out. I leafed through it. There were some dictations, some summaries and an essay.

Describe what you did on Sunday.

On Sunday my papa came home. My papa lives in America a lot and he comes back every now and again. He's got a villa with a swimming pool and a diving board and there are little wash-bears there. They live in the garden. I must go there. He lives in America because of his job and when he comes back he always brings me presents. This time he brought me some tennis racket things that you put under your feet so you can walk on the snow. Without them you sink in and you might even die. When I go to the mountains I will have to use them when I walk on the snow. Papa told me these rackets are used by the Eskimos. The Eskimos live on the ice at the North Pole and they have ice houses too. Inside they don't have a fridge because it wouldn't be any use. They eat a lot of seals and sometimes penguins. He said he will take me there one day. I asked him if Peppino can come too. Peppino is our gardener and he has to cut all the plants and when it is winter he has to take all the leaves off the lawn. Peppino is at least a hundred years old and as soon as he sees a plant he cuts it. He gets very tired and in the evening he has to put his feet in hot water. If he comes with us to the North Pole he won't have to do anything there, there are no plants there only snow and he can rest. Papa said he'll have to think about whether Peppino can come with us. After going to the airport me, my papa and my mama went to eat at the restaurant. They talked about where I will have to do middle school. Whether I'll have to live in Pavia or in America. I didn't say anything but I prefer Pavia where all my friends go. In America I can play with the little wash-bears. After lunch we went home I had another meal and went to bed. That's what I did on Sunday. I had already done my homework on Saturday.

I closed Filippo's exercise book and put it in the folder. At the bottom of the suitcase there was a rolled-up towel. I opened it and inside there was a pistol. I stared at it. It was big, it had a wooden butt and it was black. I lifted it. It was very heavy. Maybe it was loaded. I put it back.

'Over the field I chased a dragonfly, forgetting all the cares of days gone by,' they were singing on the radio.

Mama was dancing and meanwhile she was ironing and singing along. 'Just when I thought that all was well I fell.'

She was in a good mood. For a week she had been worse than a mad dog and now she was singing away happily in her hoarse, masculine voice: 'A foolish phrase, a vulgar pun, alarmed me…'

I came out of my bedroom buttoning up my shorts. She smiled at me. 'Here he is! The boy who wouldn't sleep with guests…Good morning! Come and give me a kiss. A real smacker. The biggest kiss you can.'

'Will you catch me?'

'Yes. I'll catch you.'

I took a run-up and jumped into her arms and she

caught me in mid-air and planted a kiss on my cheek. Then she hugged me and whirled me round. I gave her lots of kisses too.

'Me too! Me too!' shrieked Maria. She threw her dolls in the air and clung on to us.

'It's my turn. It's my turn. Get off,' I said to her.

'Michele, don't be like that.' Mama picked up Maria too. 'Both together!' And she started dancing round the room singing at the top of her voice. 'The store has many boxes in a stack, some red, some yellow, and some others black…'

From one side to the other. From one side to the other. Till we collapsed on the sofa.

'Feel. My heart. Feel my heart…Feel your mother's…heart…die.' She was out of breath. We put our hands on her bosom, there was a drum underneath.

We lay close together, slumped on the cushions. Then mama straightened her hair and asked me, 'Didn't Sergio eat you last night then?'

'No.'

'Did he let you sleep?'

'Yes.'

'Did he snore?'

'Yes.'

'How did he snore? Show me.'

I tried to imitate him.

'But that's a pig! That's the noise pigs make. Maria, show us how papa snores.'

And Maria imitated papa.

'You're no good, either of you. I'll do papa for you.'

She did a perfect imitation. Whistle and all.

We laughed a lot.

She got up and pulled her dress down. 'I'll warm the milk for you.'

I asked her, 'Where's papa?'

'He's gone out with Sergio…He said he's going to take us to the seaside next week. And we'll go to the restaurant and eat mussels.'

Maria and I started jumping up and down on the sofa. 'The seaside! The seaside! To eat mussels!'

Mama looked towards the fields then closed the shutters. 'Let's hope so, anyway.'

I had breakfast. There was sponge cake. I had two slices dunked in milk. Without letting anyone see, I cut another slice, wrapped it in my napkin and put it in my pocket.

Filippo would be pleased.

Mama cleared away. 'As soon as you've finished, take this cake to Salvatore's house. Put on a clean T-shirt.'

Mama was a good cook. And when she made cakes or maccheroni al forno or bread, she always made some extra and sold it to Salvatore's mother.

I cleaned my teeth, put on my Olympic Games T-shirt and went out carrying the baking tin.

There was no wind. The sun was beating down on the houses from directly overhead.

Maria was sitting on the steps with her Barbie, in a patch of shade. 'Do you know how to build a dolls' house?'

'Sure.' I had never done it, but it couldn't be difficult. 'In papa's truck there's a big box. We can cut it up and make a house out of it. And then paint it. I haven't got time now, though. I've got to go round to Salvatore's house.' I went on down to the street.

There was nobody around. Only the hens scratching about in the dust and the swallows darting under the eaves.

Some noises were coming from the big shed. I went towards it. Felice's 127 had its bonnet up and was tilted on one side. A pair of large black army boots stuck out from underneath.

When Felice was at Acqua Traverse he was always tinkering with the car. He washed it. He oiled it. He dusted it. He had even painted a wide black stripe on top of it, like the ones on American police cars. He would take the engine to pieces and then not be able to put it back together again or he would lose a bolt and then make us go to Lucignano to buy him one.

'Michele! Michele, come here!' Felice shouted from under the car.

I stopped. 'What do you want?'

'Help me.'

'I can't. I've got to do an errand for my mother.' I wanted to give the cake to Salvatore's mother, jump on the Crock and dash off to see Filippo.

'Come here.'

'I can't…I've got to do something.'

He growled. 'If you don't come here, I'll kill you…'

'What do you want?'

'I'm stuck. I can't move. A wheel came off while I was underneath, fuck it. I've been under here nearly half an hour!'

I looked inside the bonnet, from above the engine I could see the grease-blackened face and the red, desperate eyes. 'Shall I go and call your father?'

Felice's father had been a mechanic when he was young. And when Felice messed about with the car he always flew into a rage.

'Are you crazy? He'd beat the shit out of me…Help me.'

I could go off and leave him there. I looked around.

'Don't even think it…I'll get out of here and I'll snap you like a stick of liquorice. All that'll be left of you will be a grave for your parents to take flowers to,' said Felice.

'What do you want me to do?'

'Get the jack from behind the car and put it by the wheel.'

I put it there and turned the handle. Slowly the car lifted.

Felice moaned with joy. 'That's the way. That's right, so I can get out. Well done!'

He slid out. His shirt was smeared with black oil. He ran his hand through his hair. 'I thought I'd had it. I've done my back in. All because of that fucking Roman!' He started doing press-ups, swearing all the while.

'The old man?'

'Yeah, I hate his guts.' He got up and kicked the sacks of corn. 'I told him I can't get up there by car. That road ruins my shock absorbers, but he doesn't give a shit. Why doesn't *he* go up there in his fucking Mercedes? Why doesn't he stay up there? I can't take any more of this. And it's don't do this and don't do that. He chewed my balls off because I went to the seaside a couple of times. It was much better when that piece of shit wasn't here. But I'm getting out…' He punched the tractor and vented his anger by smashing up the wooden crates. 'If he calls me an idiot one more time I'm going to hit him so hard he'll stick to the

wall. And now how the fuck am I going to get up there…'
He stopped short when he remembered I was there too.
He grabbed me by the T-shirt and lifted me up and shoved
his nose in my face. 'You tell no one what I've told you, got
it? If I find out you've breathed one word of this I'll cut off
your cock and eat it with broccoli…' He took a knife from
his pocket. The blade flicked out to within two centimetres
of my nose. 'Got it?'

I stammered: 'Got it.'

He threw me down on the ground. 'No one! Now get
lost.' And he started pacing round the shed.

I picked up the cake and got the hell out of there.

The Scardaccione family was the richest in Acqua Traverse.

Salvatore's father, the Avvocato Emilio Scardaccione,
owned a lot of land. Large numbers of people worked for
him, especially at harvest time. They came from outside.
From far away. On trucks. On foot.

Papa, too, for many years, before he became a truck
driver, had gone to do seasonal work for the Avvocato
Scardaccione.

To enter Salvatore's house you went through a wrought-
iron gate, crossed a courtyard with square bushes, a very
tall palm tree and a stone fountain with goldfish in it, went
up a marble stairway with high steps and you were there.

As soon as you entered you found yourself in a dark,
windowless corridor, so long you could have cycled down
it. On one side was a row of bedrooms that were always
locked, on the other was the hall. This was a big room with
angels painted on the ceiling and a large shiny table with

chairs round it. Between two pictures with golden frames there was a display case containing some valuable cups and glasses and some photographs of men in uniform. Near the front door stood the medieval suit of armour holding a mace with a ball bristling with nails. The Avvocato had bought it in the town of Gubbio. You couldn't touch it because it was liable to fall over.

In the daytime the shutters were never opened. Not even during the winter. There was a musty atmosphere, a smell of old wood. It was like being in a church.

Signora Scardaccione, Salvatore's mother, was very fat and barely five foot high and wore a net over her hair. Her legs were swollen like sausages and always hurt and she only went out at Christmas and Easter to go to the hairdresser's in Lucignano. She spent her life in the kitchen, the only well-lit room in the house, with her sister, Aunt Lucilla, amid the steam and the smell of ragù.

They were like a pair of seals. They bowed their heads together, laughed together, clapped their hands together. Two large trained seals with perms. They sat all day long in two armchairs which they had worn out checking that Antonia, the maid, wasn't making any mistakes or taking too long rests.

Everything had to be neat and tidy for when the Avvocato Scardaccione came back from town. But he hardly ever did come back. And when he did he couldn't wait to get away again.

'Lucilla! Lucilla, look who's here!' said Letizia Scardaccione when she saw me enter the kitchen.

Aunt Lucilla raised her head from the sewing machine and smiled. On her nose she had some thick specs that made her eyes as small as a fisherman's sinkers. 'Michele! Michele, darling! What have you brought, the cake?'

'Yes, Signora. Here it is.' I delivered it to her.

'Give it to Antonia.'

Antonia was sitting at the table stuffing peppers.

Antonia Ammirati was eighteen, she was thin but not excessively so. She had red hair and blue eyes and when she was small her parents had been killed in a road accident.

I went over to Antonia and gave her the cake. She stroked my head with the back of her hand.

I was very keen on Antonia, she was beautiful and I would have liked to go out with her, but she was too old and she had a boyfriend in Lucignano who put up television aerials.

'Isn't your mama a clever lady?' said Letizia Scardaccione.

'And isn't she beautiful?' added Aunt Lucilla.

'And you're a very handsome little boy. Isn't he, Lucilla?'

'Very handsome.'

'Antonia, isn't Michele handsome? If he was grown up wouldn't you marry him?'

Antonia laughed. 'Like a shot, I would.'

Aunt Lucilla took a pinch of my cheek and almost pulled it off. 'And would you marry Antonia?'

I went all red and shook my head.

The two sisters shrieked with laughter, and went on and on.

Then Letizia Scardaccione picked up a bag. 'I've got some clothes here that are too small for Salvatore. Take them. If the trousers are too long I'll shorten them for you. Do take them, I'd be very pleased if you did. Just look at the state you're in.'

I would have liked to. They were practically new. But mama said we didn't accept charity from anyone. Especially not from those two. She said my clothes were perfectly all right. And she would decide when it was time to change them. 'Thank you, Signora. But I can't.'

Aunt Lucilla opened a tin box and clapped her hands. 'Look what I've got here. Honey drops! Do you like honey drops?'

'Yes, I do, very much, Signora.'

'Help yourself.'

These I could take. Mama never found out because I always ate the lot. I took a good supply. I filled my pockets with them.

Letizia Scardaccione added, 'And give some to your sister too. Next time you come bring her as well.'

I repeated like a parrot. 'Thank you, thank you, thank you…'

'Before you go, pop in and say hello to Salvatore. He's in his room. Don't stay too long though, he's got to practise. He has his lesson today.'

I went out of the kitchen and crossed that gloomy corridor, with that black, sombre furniture. I passed Nunzio's bedroom. The door was locked.

Once I had found it open and had gone in.

There was nothing in there, except a high bed with iron railings and some leather straps. In the middle the floor tiles were all scored and broken. When you passed the villa you used to see Nunzio walking backwards and forwards, from the door to the window.

The Avvocato had done all he could to cure him. Once he had even taken him to see Padre Pio, but Nunzio had grabbed hold of a Madonna and knocked her over and the friars had thrown him out of the church. Since he had been in the mental hospital he had never been back to Acqua Traverse.

I must go and see Filippo, I had promised. I must take him the cake and the sweets. But it was hot. He could wait. It wouldn't make any difference to him. Besides, I felt like spending a bit of time with Salvatore.

I heard the piano through his bedroom door. I knocked.

'Who is it?'

'Michele.'

'Michele?' He opened the door, looked around like a hunted criminal, pushed me inside and locked the door.

Salvatore's room was big and bare, with high ceilings. Against one wall there was an upright piano. Along another a bed so high you needed a little stepladder to get onto it. And a long bookcase with lots of books in it arranged according to the colour of their covers. The games were kept in a chest of drawers. A heavy white curtain let through a ray of sunlight in which the dust danced.

In the middle of the room, on the floor, was the green Subbuteo cloth. Laid out on it were Juventus and Torino.

'What are you doing here?'

'Nothing much. I brought a cake. Can I stay? Your mother said you've got your lesson…'

'Yes, you stay,' he lowered his voice, 'but if they notice I'm not playing they won't leave me in peace.' He picked up a record and put it on the record player. 'This'll make them think I'm playing.' And he added with a very serious air, 'It's Chopin.'

'Who's Chopin?'

'He's one of the best.'

Salvatore and I were the same age, but to me he seemed older. Partly because he was taller than I was, partly because he had white shirts that were always clean and long trousers with a crease in them. Partly because of his placid way of speaking. They forced him to play the piano, a teacher came once a week from Lucignano to give him lessons and, although he hated music, he didn't complain and he always added, 'But when I grow up I'll stop.'

'How about a game?' I asked him.

Subbuteo was my favourite game. I wasn't very good at it, but I really enjoyed it. In the winter Salvatore and I had endless tournaments, we spent whole afternoons flicking those little plastic footballers around. Salvatore played on his own too. He would move from one end to the other. If he wasn't playing Subbuteo he would be lining up thousands of soldiers round the room and covering the whole floor till there wasn't even room for your feet. And when they were all finally set out in geometric formations he would start moving them one by one. He would spend hours in silence arranging armies, and then, when Antonia came to say that dinner was served, he would put them all back in the shoeboxes.

'Look,' he said, and took out of a drawer eight small green cardboard boxes. Each box contained a football team. 'Look what papa gave me. He brought me them from Rome.'

'All these?' I picked them up. The Avvocato must be really rich to spend all that money.

Every single year, on my birthday and at Christmas, I asked papa and Baby Jesus to give me Subbuteo, but it was no use, neither of them heard. Just one team would have been enough. Without the pitch and the goals. Even a Serie B team. I would have liked to go round to Salvatore's with my own team because, I was sure, if it was mine I would play better, I wouldn't lose so much. I would have adored those players, I would have taken care of them and I would have beaten Salvatore.

He already had four. And now his father had bought him another eight.

Why didn't I get anything?

Because my father didn't care about me, he said he loved me but he didn't. He had given me a stupid Venetian boat to put on the television set. And I couldn't even touch it.

I wanted a team. If his father had given him four I wouldn't have said anything, but he'd given him eight. He had twelve now, altogether.

What difference would one less make to him?

I cleared my throat and whispered, 'Will you give me one of them?'

Salvatore frowned and started pacing round the room. Then he said, 'I'm sorry, I would give you one, but I can't. If papa found out I'd given it to you he'd be angry.'

That wasn't true. When had his father ever checked up on the teams? Salvatore was stingy.

'I see.'

'Anyway, what difference does it make? You can come and play with them whenever you like.'

If I'd had something to swap, perhaps he would had given me one. But I didn't have anything.

Wait a minute, I did have something to swap.

'If I tell you a secret, will you give me one?'

Salvatore gave me a sidelong glance. 'What secret?'

'An incredible secret.'

'No secret's worth a team.'

'Mine is.' I kissed my forefingers. 'I swear.'

'What if it's just a trick?'

'It's not. But if you say it's a trick I'll give the team back to you.'

'I'm not interested in secrets.'

'I know. But this is a great one. I haven't told it to anybody. If Skull found out, he'd be over the moon…'

'Tell it to Skull then.'

But now I would stoop to anything. 'I'll even take Lanerossi Vicenza.'

Salvatore goggled. 'Lanerossi Vicenza?'

'Yes.'

We loathed Lanerossi Vicenza. They had a jinx on them. If you played with them you always lost. Neither of us had ever won with that team. And it had one player that had lost its head, another that had been stuck on with glue and a goalkeeper that was all bent.

Salvatore thought it over for a while and finally conceded. 'All right. But if it's a crappy secret I'm not giving it to you.'

And so I told him everything. About when I had fallen out of the tree. About the hole. About Filippo. About when he was crazy. About his bad leg. About the stink. About Felice keeping guard over him. About papa and the old man wanting to cut off his ears. About Francesco throwing himself off a cliff with his pecker out. About his mother being on television.

Everything.

It was a wonderful feeling. Like the time I had eaten a jarful of peaches in syrup. Afterwards I had been ill, I felt as if I was bursting, I had an earthquake in my stomach and I had even got a temperature and mama had first boxed my ears then put my head down the toilet and stuck two fingers in my throat. And I had brought up an enormous amount of yellow acid gunk. And had started living again.

While I talked Salvatore listened silently, impassively.

And I concluded, 'And then he's always talking about little wash-bears. Little bears that wash clothes. I told him they don't exist, but he won't listen to me.'

'Little wash-bears do exist.'

I gaped. 'What do you mean they do exist? My father said they don't.'

'They live in America.' He got out the *Great Encyclopaedia of Animals* and leafed through it. 'There it is. Look.' He passed me the book.

There was a colour photograph of a sort of fox. With a white muzzle and a little black mask over its eyes like Zorro. But it was furrier than a fox and had smaller legs and could pick things up with them. It had an apple in its hands. It was a very pretty little animal. 'So they do exist...'

'Yes.' Salvatore read: 'A bearlike carnivorous genus of the Procyonidae family, with a rather plump body, a pointed muzzle and a large head, and big eyes surrounded by brownish-black patches. Its fur is grey and its tail not very long. It lives in Canada and the United States. It is commonly known as the little wash-bear because of its curious habit of washing food before eating it.'

'It's not clothes they wash, it's food…Oh.' I was shaken. 'And I told him they didn't exist…'

'And why do they keep him in there?' Salvatore asked.

'Because they don't want to give him back to his mother.' I grabbed his arm. 'Do you want to come and see him? We can go there straight away. Would you like to? I know a short-cut…It won't take long.'

He didn't answer me. He put the footballers back in their boxes and rolled up the Subbuteo pitch.

'Well? Would you like to?'

He turned the key and opened the door. 'I can't. My teacher's coming. If I haven't done my exercises he'll tell those two women and I'll never hear the end of it.'

'What do you mean? Don't you want to see him? Didn't you like my secret?'

'Not much. I'm not interested in loonies in holes.'

'Will you give me Vicenza?'

'Take them. They're rubbish anyway.' He thrust the box into my hand and pushed me out of the room. And shut the door.

I pedalled towards the hill and I didn't understand.

How could he not care less about a boy chained up in a hole? Salvatore had said my secret was rubbish.

I shouldn't have told him. I had wasted my secret. And what had I got out of it? Lanerossi Vicenza, the jinx team.

I was worse than Judas who had bartered Jesus for thirty pieces of silver. With thirty pieces of silver just think how many teams you could buy.

I was carrying the box stuffed inside my shorts. It was bothering me. The corners stuck into my skin. I wanted to throw it away, but couldn't bring myself to do it.

I wished I could turn the clock back. I would have given the cake to Signora Scardaccione and gone away, without even calling on Salvatore.

I went up the slope so fast that when I got there I felt sick.

I had ditched my bike just before the slope and covered the last part on foot, running through the wheat. I felt as if my heart was tearing out of my chest. I wanted to go straight to Filippo, but I had to flop down under a tree and wait till I got my breath back.

When I felt better, I looked to see if Felice was around. There was nobody. I climbed into the house and got the rope.

I moved the corrugated sheet and called out to him. 'Filippo!'

'Michele!' He started moving about. He was waiting for me.

'I've come. You see? You see? I've come.'

'I knew you would.'

'Did the little wash-bears tell you?'

'No. I knew you would. You promised.'

'You're right, the little wash-bears do exist. I read about it in a book. I've even seen a photograph of one.'

'Cute, aren't they?'

'Very cute. Have you ever seen one?'

'Yes. Can you hear them? Can you hear them whistling?'

I couldn't hear any whistling. There were no two

ways about it, he was crazy.

'Are you coming?' He beckoned me down.

I grabbed the rope. 'Yes, I'm coming.' I lowered myself down.

They had cleaned up. The bucket was empty. The little saucepan was full of water. Filippo was wrapped in his disgusting blanket, but they had washed it. They had bound up his ankle with a bandage. And he no longer had the chain round his foot.

'They've cleaned you!'

He smiled. They hadn't cleaned his teeth.

'Who was it?'

He kept one hand over his eyes. 'The lord of the worms and his dwarf servants. They came down and they washed me all over. I told them they could wash me as much as they liked but you would catch them anyway and they could run away as far as they wanted but you could follow them for several kilometres without getting tired.'

I grabbed his wrist. 'You didn't tell them my name, did you?'

'What name?'

'My name.'

'What is your name?'

'Michele…'

'Michele? No!'

'But you just called me…'

'Your name's not Michele.'

'What is my name?'

'Dolores.'

'My name's not Dolores. It's Michele Amitrano.'

'If you say so.' I had a feeling he was pulling my leg.

'But what did you tell the lord of the worms?'

'I told him the guardian angel would catch them.'

I breathed a sigh of relief. 'Oh, thank goodness! You told him I was the guardian angel.' I took the cake out of my pocket. 'Look what I've brought you. It's crumbled…' I didn't even have time to finish the sentence before he pounced on me.

He snatched what was left of the cake and stuffed it in his mouth, then, with his eyes closed, he searched for the crumbs.

He fumbled all over me. 'More! More! Give me more!' He scratched me with his nails.

'I haven't got any more. I swear. Hang on…' In my back pocket I had the sweets. 'Here. Take these.'

He unwrapped them, chewed them and swallowed them at an incredible rate.

'More! More!'

'I've given you the lot.'

He wouldn't believe I didn't have anything else. He kept searching for the crumbs.

'Tomorrow I'll bring you some more. What do you want?'

He scratched his head. 'I want…I want…some bread. Bread and butter. Butter and marmalade. With ham. And cheese. And chocolate. A really big sandwich.'

'I'll see what there is at home.'

I sat down. Filippo wouldn't stop touching my feet and untying my sandals.

Suddenly I had an idea. A great idea.

He didn't have the chain. He was free. I could take him out.

I asked him, 'Do you want to go out?'

'Out where?'

'Outside.'

'Outside?'

'Yes, outside. Outside the hole.'

He fell silent for a moment, then he asked, 'Hole? What hole?'

'This hole. In here. Where we are.'

He shook his head. 'There aren't any holes.'

'This isn't a hole?'

'No.'

'Yes it is a hole, you said so yourself.'

'When did I say so?'

'You said that the world's all full of holes with dead people in them. And that the moon's full of holes too.'

'You're wrong. I didn't say that.'

I was beginning to lose patience. 'Well where are we, then?'

'In a place where you wait.'

'And what do you wait for?'

'To go to heaven.'

In a way he was right. If you stayed there all your life, you would die and then your soul would fly to heaven. If you got into a discussion with Filippo your thoughts got tangled.

'Come on, I'll take you out. Come with me.' I took his hand, but he stiffened and trembled. 'All right. All right. We won't go out. Keep calm, though. I won't hurt you.'

He stuck his head under the blanket. 'Outside there's no air. Outside I'll suffocate. I don't want to go out there.'

'No you won't. There's loads of air outside. I'm always

outside and I don't suffocate. How do you think that's possible?'

'You're an angel.'

I must get him to see reason. 'Listen carefully. Yesterday I swore to you I'd come back and I have come back. Now I swear to you that if you come out nothing will happen to you. You've got to believe me.'

'Why do I have to go outside? I'm all right in here.'

I had to tell him a lie. 'Because heaven's outside. And I've got to take you to heaven. I'm an angel and you're dead and I've got to take you to heaven.'

He thought about this for a while. 'Really?'

'Truly.'

'Let's go, then.' And he started making high-pitched squeaks.

I tried to get him to his feet, but he kept his legs bent. He couldn't support himself. If I didn't hold him up he fell down. Finally I tied the rope round his hips. Then I wrapped his head in the blanket, so that he would keep quiet. I went back up and started hoisting him. He was too heavy. He hung there, twenty centimetres off the ground, all stiff and crooked, and me on top, with the rope over my shoulder, bent right forward and without the strength to pull him up.

'Help me, Filippo. I can't do it.'

But he was like a lead weight and the rope was slipping out of my hands. I stepped back and the rope slackened. He had touched the bottom.

I looked down. He had keeled over on his back with the blanket on his head.

'Filippo, are you all right?'

'Am I there?' he asked.

'Hang on.' I ran round the house looking for a plank, a pole, something that could help me. In the cowshed I found a battered old door with the paint flaking off it. I dragged it into the yard. I wanted to lower it into the hole and get Filippo to climb up it. I stood it on the edge of the hole, but I dropped it on the ground and it split into two halves full of sharp splinters. The wood was all worm-eaten. It was no good.

'Michele?' Filippo was calling me.

'Wait a minute! Just a minute!' I shouted, and I picked up a piece of that damned door, lifted it over my head and threw it on top of a ladder.

A ladder?

There it was, two metres away from the hole. A beautiful green-painted wooden ladder lying on the ivy that covered a pile of masonry and earth. It had been there all the time and I hadn't seen it. That was how they got down.

'I've found a ladder!' I said to Filippo. I fetched it and lowered it into the hole.

I dragged him into the wood, under a tree. There were birds. Cicadas. Shade. And there was a pleasant smell of damp earth and moss.

I asked him, 'Can I take the blanket off your face?'

'Are we in the sun?'

'No.'

He didn't want to take it off, but eventually I persuaded him to let me blindfold him with my T-shirt. He was pleased, you could tell from the way he smiled. A light breeze caressed his skin and he was really enjoying it.

I asked him, 'Why did they put you here?'

'I don't know. I can't remember.'

'Not anything?'

'I found myself here.'

'What *do* you remember?'

'I was at school.' He lolled his head to and fro. 'I remember that. We had gym. Then I went out. A white car pulled up. And I found myself here.'

'But where do you live?'

'In Via Modigliani 36. On the corner of Via Cavalier D'Arpino.

'Where's that?'

'In Pavia.'

'In Italy?'

'Yes.'

'This is Italy too.'

He stopped talking. I thought he had fallen asleep, but after a while he asked me: 'What sort of birds are these?'

I looked around. 'Sparrows.'

'Are you sure they're not bats?'

'No. Bats sleep in the daytime and they make a different noise.'

'Flying foxes fly even in the daytime and they chirp like birds. And they weigh more than a kilo. If they catch hold of the small branches they fall to the ground. I think these are flying foxes.'

After the little wash-bear business I thought I had better keep quiet, maybe in America they had flying foxes too. I asked him, 'Have you ever been to America?'

'Yesterday I saw my mother. She told me she can't come

and get me because she's dead. She's dead with all my family. Otherwise, she said, she would come straight away.'

I stopped up my ears.

'Filippo, it's late. I've got to take you down.'

'Can I really go back down?'

'Yes.'

'All right. Let's go back.'

He had been mute for half an hour, with the T-shirt tied over his eyes. Every now and then his neck and mouth stiffened and his fingers and toes contracted as if he had a tic. He had been sitting spellbound, quite still, listening to the flying foxes.

'Hold on to my neck.' He clung on and I dragged him to the hole. 'Now we'll go down the ladder, hold tight. Don't let go of me.'

It was difficult. Filippo squeezed so hard that I couldn't breathe and I couldn't see the rungs of the ladder, I had to feel for them with my feet.

When we got to the bottom I was as white as a sheet and panting. I put him in a corner. I covered him up and gave him a drink and said to him, 'It's very late. I must get going. Papa'll kill me.'

'I'll stay here. But you must bring me the sandwiches. And a roast chicken too.'

'We have chicken on Sundays. Today mama's making meatballs. Do you like meatballs?'

'In tomato sauce?'

'Yes.'

'I like them very much.'

I was sorry to leave him. 'I'll be off, then…' I was about to grab a rung, when the ladder was pulled away.

I looked up.

On the edge of the hole was a man with a brown hood over his head. He was dressed exactly like a soldier. 'Cuckoo? Cuckoo? April now is through,' he sang and started pirouetting. 'Maytime has returned to the song of the cuckoo. Guess who?'

'Felice!'

'Well done!' he said, and fell silent for a bit. 'How the fuck did you guess? Hang on. Hang on a minute.'

He went off and when he reappeared he had his rifle over his shoulder.

'It was you!' Felice clapped his hands. 'It was you, fuck it all! I kept finding things arranged differently. At first I thought I was crazy. Then I thought it must be a ghost. And all the time it was you. Little Michele. Thank God for that, I was going out of my mind.'

I felt my ankle being squeezed. Filippo had caught hold of my feet and was whispering: 'The lord of the worms comes and goes. The lord of the worms comes and goes. The lord of the worms comes and goes.'

So that was who the lord of the worms was!

Felice looked at me through the holes in his hood. 'Made friends with the prince, have you? See how well I washed him? He put up a bit of a struggle, but I won in the end. Wouldn't give me the blanket, though.'

I was trapped. I couldn't see him. The sun filtering through the foliage blinded me.

'Cop this!'

A knife sank into the ground. Ten centimetres away from my sandal and twenty from Filippo's head.

'How about that for accuracy? I could have sliced your big toe off just like that. And what would you have done then?'

I couldn't speak. My throat was blocked up.

'What would you have done without a toe?' he repeated. 'Tell me. Come on, tell me.'

'I'd have bled to death.'

'Good boy. And if I shoot you with this,' he showed me the rifle, 'what happens to you?'

'I die.'

'You see you do know things. Come on up, move!' Felice got the ladder and lowered it down.

I didn't want to, but I had no choice. He would shoot me. I wasn't sure I would be able to climb up, my legs were shaking.

'Hang on, hang on,' said Felice. 'Pick up my knife.'

I bent down and Filippo whispered, 'Won't you be coming back again?'

I pulled the knife out of the earth and, without letting Felice see, replied in a low voice, 'I'll be back.'

'Promise?'

'Close it up and put it in your pocket,' Felice ordered.

'Promise.'

'Come on, come on! Up you get, you little runt. What're you waiting for?'

I started climbing. Filippo meanwhile kept whispering. 'The lord of the worms comes and goes. The lord of the worms comes and goes. The lord of the worms comes and goes.'

When I was almost out, Felice grabbed me by the trousers and with both hands threw me against the house like a sack. I crashed into the wall and crumpled on the ground. I tried to get up. I had banged my side. A spasm of pain stiffened my leg and arm. I turned. Felice had taken off his hood and was charging towards me pointing the rifle at me. I saw his tank-like boots growing bigger and bigger.

Now he's going to shoot me, I thought.

I started crawling, all aches and pains, towards the wood.

'Thought you'd set him free, did you? Well you were wrong. You counted your chickens before they hatched.' He gave me a kick in the backside. 'Get up, you little shit. What are you doing down there on the ground? Get up! Haven't hurt yourself, have you?' He lifted me up by the ear. 'You can thank your lucky stars you're your father's son. Otherwise by this time…Now I'm going to take you home. Your father'll decide your punishment. I've done my duty. I've kept guard. And I ought to have shot you.'

He dragged me into the wood. I was so scared I couldn't cry. I kept tripping over and falling on the ground and he kept pulling me up again by the ear. 'Move, go, go, go!'

We emerged from the trees.

In front of us the yellow incandescent expanse of wheat stretched as far as the sky. If I dived in he would never find me.

With the barrel of his rifle Felice pushed me towards the 127 and said, 'Oh yes, give me back my knife!'

I tried to give it to him but couldn't get my hand in my pocket.

'I'll do it!' He took it. He opened the door, lifted the

seat and said, 'Get in!'

I got in and there was Salvatore.

'Salvatore, what are you…' The rest died in my mouth.

It had been Salvatore. He had ratted to Felice.

Salvatore looked at me and turned away.

I sat down in the back without saying a word.

Felice got behind the wheel. 'Salvatore old boy, you've done a really good job. Allow me to shake your hand.' Felice grasped it. 'You were right, the nosey parker was there. And I didn't believe you.' He got out. 'A promise is a promise. And when Felice Natale makes a promise, he keeps it. You drive. Take it slowly, though.'

'Now?' Salvatore asked.

'When else? Get into my seat.'

Felice got in at the passenger's door and Salvatore moved over to the wheel. 'It's perfect for learning here. All you have to do is follow the slope and brake now and again.'

Salvatore Scardaccione had sold me for a driving lesson.

'You'll smash the car up if you don't watch out!' Felice shouted and with his head up against the windscreen he watched the broken surface of the road. 'Brake! Brake!'

Salvatore could hardly see over the steering wheel and gripped it as if he wanted to break it.

When Felice had come towards me pointing his rifle at me I had pissed myself. I hadn't noticed till now. My underpants were soaked.

The car was full of crazed horseflies. We bounced on the humps, we plunged into the holes. I had to cling on to the door handle.

Salvatore had never told me he wanted to drive a car. He could have asked his father to teach him. The Avvocato never refused him anything. Why had he asked Felice?

My whole body was hurting, my skinned knees, my ribs, my arm and my wrist. But especially my heart. Salvatore had broken it.

He was my best friend. Once, on a branch of the carob, we had even made a vow of eternal friendship. We used to go home from school together. If one of us got out earlier he would wait for the other.

Salvatore had betrayed me.

Mama was right when she said the Scardacciones thought they were it just because they had money. And she said that even if you were drowning they wouldn't lift a finger to help you. And dozens of times I had imagined the two Scardaccione sisters on the edge of the quicksands beavering away on their sewing machine and me sinking and stretching out my hand and calling for help and them throwing me honey drops and saying they couldn't get up because of their swollen legs. But Salvatore and I were friends.

I had been wrong.

I felt a dreadful urge to cry, but I swore to myself that if a single tear came out of my eyes, I would take the old man's pistol and shoot myself. I pulled the Lanerossi Vicenza box out of my shorts. It was all soaked in pee.

I put it on the seat.

Felice shouted: 'That's it, stop! I can't stand any more of this.'

Salvatore braked abruptly, the engine stalled, the car jerked to a halt and if Felice hadn't put his arms out he would have cracked his head on the windscreen.

He opened the door and got out. 'Move!'

Salvatore moved over to the other side, without a word.

Felice grasped the wheel and said, 'Salvatore old boy, I must be frank with you, you're just not cut out for driving. Forget it. Your future lies in cycling.'

When we drove into Acqua Traverse my sister, Barbara, Remo and Skull were playing hopscotch in the dust.

They saw us and stopped playing.

Papa's truck wasn't there. Nor was the old man's car.

Felice parked the 127 in the shed.

Salvatore shot out of the car, got his bike and rode off without even looking at me.

Felice pulled up the seat. 'Get out!'

I didn't want to get out.

Once, at school, I had broken the glass door to the courtyard with one of those sticks they use for gymnastics. I wanted to show Angelo Cantini, a classmate of mine, that the glass was indestructible. Instead, it had shattered into a billion neat little cubes. The headmaster had called mama and told her he had to speak to her.

When she arrived she had looked at me and said in my ear, 'I'll deal with you later.' And she had gone into the headmaster's room while I sat waiting in the corridor.

I had been scared then, but that was nothing to what I felt now. Felice would tell mama everything and she would tell papa. And papa would be very angry. And the old man would take me away.

'Get out!' Felice repeated.

I summoned up all my courage and got out.

I was embarrassed. My trousers were wet.

Barbara put her hand to her mouth. Remo ran over to Skull. Maria took off her glasses and wiped them on her T-shirt.

The light was dazzling, I couldn't keep my eyes open. Behind me I could hear Felice's heavy footsteps. Barbara's mother was looking out of the window. Skull's mother was looking out of another. They gazed at me with vacant eyes. There would have been complete silence if Togo hadn't started barking his shrill little bark. Skull gave him a kick and Togo fled yelping.

I went up the front steps and opened the door.

The shutters were closed and there wasn't much light. The radio was on. The fan was spinning. Mama, in her petticoat, was sitting at the table peeling potatoes. She saw me come in followed by Felice. The knife slipped out of her hand. It fell on the table, and from there dropped onto the floor.

'What's happened?'

Felice thrust his hands in his combat jacket, lowered his head and said, 'He was up there. With the boy.'

Mama got up from her chair, turned off the radio, took one step, then another, stopped, put her hands to her face and squatted down on the floor looking at me.

I burst into tears.

She ran to me and took me in her arms. She hugged me tightly to her bosom and realised I was all wet. She put me on the chair and looked at my grazed legs and arms, the clotted blood on my knees. She lifted up my T-shirt.

'What happened to you?' she asked me.

'Him! It was him…he…he beat me up!' I pointed at Felice.

Mama turned, glared at Felice and growled, 'What have you done to him, you bully?'

Felice raised his hands. 'Nothing. What have I done to him? Brought him home.'

Mama narrowed her eyes. 'You! How dare you, you?' The veins on her neck swelled and her voice shook. 'How dare you, eh? You hit my son, you bastard!' And she flung herself at Felice.

He backed away. 'So I gave him a kick up the backside. What's the big deal?'

Mama tried to slap his face. Felice held her wrists to keep her away, but she was a lioness. 'You bastard! I'll scratch your eyes out!'

'I found him in the hole…He wanted to free the boy. I hardly touched him. Stop it, calm down!'

Mama was in bare feet, but she still managed to give him a kick in the balls.

Poor Felice let out a strange noise, a cross between a gargle and the sound of water going down a plughole, put his hands to his genitals and fell to his knees. He screwed up his face with pain and tried to shout but it wouldn't come, all the air had gone from his lungs.

I, still standing on the chair, stopped blubbing. I knew how much a bang in the nuts hurt. And that was a very hard bang in the nuts.

Mama had no mercy. She picked up the frying pan out of the sink and slammed Felice in the face. He howled and collapsed on the floor.

Mama raised the frying pan again, she wanted to kill

him, but Felice caught her by the ankle and pulled. Mama fell down. The frying pan shot across the floor. Felice threw himself on top of her with his whole body.

I whimpered in despair. 'Leave her alone! Leave her alone! Leave her alone!' Felice gripped her arms, sat on her stomach and held her still.

Mama bit and scratched like a cat. Her petticoat had ridden up. You could see her bottom and the black tuft between her legs and a shoulder strap had snapped and one breast was coming out, white and big and with a dark nipple.

Felice stopped and looked at her.

I saw how he looked at her.

I got off the chair and tried to kill him. I jumped on him and did my best to throttle him.

At that moment papa and the old man came in.

Papa threw himself on Felice, grabbed him by the arm and pulled him off mama.

Felice rolled over on the ground and I rolled over with him.

I banged my temple hard. A kettle started whistling in my head, and in my nostrils I had the smell of that disinfectant they use in the school toilets. Yellow lights exploded in front of my eyes.

Papa was kicking Felice and Felice was crawling under the table and the old man was trying to restrain papa who had his mouth open and was stretching out his hands and knocking over the chairs with his feet.

The hiss in my head was so loud that I couldn't

even hear my own sobs.

Mama picked me up and took me into her bedroom, shut the door with her elbow and laid me on the bed. I couldn't stop crying. My body was heaving and my face was purple.

She squeezed me in her arms and kept saying, 'Never mind. Never mind. It'll soon be better. It'll soon be better.'

While I cried I couldn't take my eyes off the photograph of Padre Pio fixed to the wardrobe. The friar was looking at me and seemed to be smiling with satisfaction.

In the kitchen papa, the old man and Felice were shouting.

Then all three of them left the house slamming the door.

And calm returned.

The doves were cooing on the roof. The sound of the fridge. The cicadas. The fan. That was silence.

Mama, with swollen eyes, got dressed, disinfected a scratch on her shoulder and washed me, dried me and put me under the sheets. She gave me a peach in syrup to eat and lay down beside me. She gave me her hand. She wasn't talking any more.

I didn't have the strength to bend a finger. I rested my forehead on her stomach and closed my eyes.

The door opened.

'How is he?'

Papa's voice. He spoke quietly, as if the doctor had told him I didn't have long to live.

Mama stroked my hair. 'He got a bang on the head. But now he's asleep.'

'And how are you?'

'Fine.'

'Sure?'

'Yes. But that ruffian had better not come into our house ever again. If he touches Michele again I'll kill him and then I'll kill you.'

'I've already sorted that out. I've got to go.'

The door closed.

Mama curled up beside me and whispered in my ear, 'When you grow up you must go away from here and never come back.'

It was night.

Mama wasn't there. Maria was sleeping next to me. The clock was ticking on the bedside table. The hands glowed yellow. The pillow smelled of papa. The white light of the kitchen crept under the door.

An argument was going on in there.

Even the Avvocato Scardaccione had arrived, from Rome. It was the first time he had ever been to our house.

That afternoon terrible things had happened. Too terrible, too immense even for anger. They had left me alone.

I wasn't worried. I felt safe. Mama had shut us in her bedroom and would never let anyone come in.

I had a lump on my head that hurt if I touched it, but otherwise I was fine. I was a bit sorry about that. As soon as they found out I wasn't ill they would put me back in the room with the old man. And I wanted to stay in their bed for ever. Without ever going out again, without ever seeing Salvatore, Felice, Filippo, anyone, ever again. Nothing would change.

I could hear the voices in the kitchen. The old man, the lawyer, the barber, Skull's father, papa. They were arguing about a phone call they had to make and what they should say.

I put my head under the pillow.

I saw the ocean of iron in a storm, breakers of nails rose and splashes of bolts struck the white bus that was sinking silently lifting its front end, and inside were the monsters thrashing about and pummelling with their fists in terror.

It was no use.

The windows were indestructible.

I opened my eyes.

'Michele, wake up.' Papa was sitting on the edge of the bed shaking my shoulder. 'I've got to talk to you.'

It was dark. But a patch of light bathed the ceiling. I couldn't see his eyes and I couldn't tell if he was angry.

In the kitchen they were still talking.

'Michele, what did you do today?'

'Nothing.'

'Don't talk nonsense.' He was angry.

'I didn't do anything wrong. I swear.'

'Felice found you with that boy. He says you wanted to free him.'

I sat up. 'No! It's not true! I swear it! I took him out, but I put him straight back in again. I didn't want to free him. He's the one who's lying.'

'Keep your voice down, your sister's asleep.' Maria was lying face down hugging the pillow.

I whispered, 'Don't you believe me?'

155

He looked at me. His eyes glittered in the dark like a dog's.

'How many times have you seen him?'

'Three.'

'How many?'

'Four.'

'Can he recognise you?'

'What?'

'If he saw you would he recognise you?'

I thought about it. 'No. He can't see. He always keeps his head under the blanket.'

'Have you told him your name?'

'No.'

'Have you spoken to him?'

'No…not much.'

'What did he say to you?'

'Nothing. He talks about strange things. I can't make head nor tail of it.'

'And what did you say to him?'

'Nothing.'

He got up. It seemed as if he wanted to go, then he sat down on the bed again. 'Listen to me carefully. I'm not joking. If you go back there I'll give you the thrashing of your life. If you go back there again those people will shoot him in the head.' He gave me a violent shake. 'And it'll be your fault.'

I stammered: 'I won't go back there again. I swear.'

'Swear it on my head.'

'I swear.'

'Say, I swear on your head that I won't go back there again.'

I said: 'I swear on your head that I won't go back there again.'

'You've sworn on the head of your father.' He sat beside me in silence.

In the kitchen Barbara's father was shouting with Felice.

Papa looked out of the window. 'Forget him. He doesn't exist any more. And you mustn't talk about him to anyone. Ever again.'

'I understand. I won't go there again.'

He lit a cigarette.

I asked him, 'Are you still cross with me?'

'No. Lie down and go to sleep.' He took a long draw and leaned with his hands on the windowsill. His shiny hair glistened in the light of the streetlamp. 'But God damn it, why is it the other boys behave themselves and you go around playing the fool?'

'So you *are* cross with me?'

'No, I'm not cross with you. Stop it.' He took his head between his hands and whispered, 'What a bloody mess.' He shook his head. 'There are things that seem wrong when you…' His voice was broken and he couldn't find the words. 'The world's wrong, Michele.'

He got up and stretched his back and made as if to leave. 'Go to sleep. I've got to go back in there.'

'Papa, will you tell me something?'

He threw the cigarette out of the window. 'What?'

'Why did you put him in the hole? I don't quite understand.'

He gripped the doorknob, I thought he wasn't going to answer me, then he said: 'Didn't you want to go away from Acqua Traverse?'

'Yes.'

'Soon we'll go and live in the city.'

'Where'll we go?'

'To the North. Are you pleased?'

I nodded.

He came back over to me and looked me in the eyes. His breath smelled of wine. 'Listen to me carefully. If you go back there they'll kill him. They've sworn it. You mustn't go back there again if you don't want them to shoot him and if you want us to go and live in the city. And you must never talk about him. Do you understand?'

'I understand.'

He kissed me on the head. 'Now go to sleep and don't think about it. Do you love your father?'

'Yes.'

'Do you want to help me?'

'Yes.'

'Then forget all about it.'

'All right.'

'Go to sleep now.' He kissed Maria, who didn't even notice, and went out of the room shutting the door quietly.

EVERYTHING WAS in disarray.

The table was covered with bottles, coffee cups and dirty plates. The flies were buzzing over the remnants of the food. The cigarettes were overflowing from the ashtray, the chairs and armchairs were all awry. There was a reek of smoke.

The door of my room was ajar. The old man was asleep fully dressed on my sister's bed. One arm hanging loose. His mouth open. Every now and then he brushed away a fly that crawled on his face. Papa had flopped down on my bed with his head against the wall. Mama was sleeping curled up on the sofa. She had covered herself with the white quilt. All you could see was her black hair, a bit of forehead and a bare foot.

The front door was open. A warm gentle draught rustled the newspaper on the chest of drawers.

The cock crowed.

I opened the fridge. I got out the milk, filled a glass and went out on the balcony. I sat down on the steps to look at the dawn.

It was bright orange, dirtied by a gelatinous, purplish mass that stretched like cotton across the horizon, but higher up the sky was clean and black and a few stars were still alight.

I finished my milk, put the glass on a step and went down into the street.

Skull's football was near the bench, I kicked it. It rolled under the old man's car.

Togo emerged from the shed. He whined and yawned simultaneously. He stretched, lengthening his body and dragging his back legs, and came towards me wagging his tail.

I kneeled down. 'Togo, how are you?'

He took my hand in his mouth and pulled it. He didn't grip tightly but his teeth were sharp.

'Where do you want to take me, eh? Where do you want to take me?' I followed him into the shed. The doves roosting on the iron rafters flew away.

In one corner, heaped on the ground, was his bed, an old grey blanket, full of holes.

'Do you want to show me your house?'

Togo lay down on it and opened out like a devilled chicken.

I knew what he wanted. I scratched his stomach and he froze, in bliss. Only his tail moved right and left.

The blanket was identical to Filippo's.

I smelled it. It didn't stink like his.

It smelled of dog.

I was lying on my bed reading *Tex*.

I had stayed in my room all day. Like when I had a

temperature and couldn't go to school. At one point Remo had dropped in to ask if I wanted a game of soccer, but I had said no, I wasn't feeling very well.

Mama had cleaned the house till everything was gleaming again, then she had gone round to see Barbara's mother. Papa and the old man had woken up and gone out.

My sister dashed into the room and jumped on her bed looking as pleased as Punch.

'Guess what Barbara lent me?'

I lowered my comic. 'I don't know.'

'Guess, go on!'

'I don't know.' I wasn't in the mood for games.

She pulled out Ken. Barbie's husband, that beanpole with the snooty expression on his face. 'Now we can play. I'll take Paola and you take him. We'll undress them and put them in the fridge…Then they can cuddle each other, you see?'

'I don't feel like it.'

She peered at me. 'What's the matter?'

'Nothing. Leave me alone, I'm reading.'

'You're so boring!' She snorted and went out.

I went on reading. It was a new number, Remo had lent it to me. But I couldn't concentrate. I threw it on the floor.

I was thinking of Filippo.

What was I going to do now? I had promised him I would go and see him again, but I couldn't, I had sworn to papa that I wouldn't go.

If I went they would shoot him.

But why? I wouldn't set him free, I would just talk to him. I wouldn't be doing anything wrong.

Filippo was waiting for me. He was there, in the hole, and was wondering when I would come back, when I would bring him the meatballs.

'I can't come,' I said out loud.

The last time I had gone to see him I had said to him, 'You see? I've come.' And he had replied that he had known I would. Not because the little wash-bears had told him. 'You promised.'

All I needed was five minutes. 'Filippo, I can't come here again. If I come back they'll kill you. I'm sorry, it's not my fault.' And at least he would know what was happening. Whereas like this he would think I didn't want to see him again and I didn't keep my promises. But that wasn't true. This tormented me.

If I couldn't go myself, papa could tell him. 'I'm sorry, Michele can't come, that's why he hasn't kept his promise. If he comes they'll kill you. He sends his regards.'

'It's no good, I must forget him!' I said to the room. I picked up the comic, went into the bathroom and started reading on the toilet, but I had to stop immediately.

Papa was calling me from the street.

What did he want from me now? I had been good, I hadn't left the house. I pulled up my trousers and went out onto the terrace.

'Come here! Quick!' He beckoned me down. He was standing beside the truck. Mama, Maria, Skull and Barbara were there too.

'What's up?'

'Come down', Mama said. 'There's a surprise.'

Filippo. Papa had freed Filippo. And he had brought him to me.

My heart stopped beating. I rushed down the stairs. 'Where is it?'

'Wait there.' Papa got onto the truck and brought out the surprise.

'Well?' papa asked me.

Mama repeated. 'Well?'

It was a red bike, with handlebars like a bull's horns. A small front wheel. Three gears. Studded tyres. A saddle long enough for two people to ride on.

Mama asked again: 'What's the matter? Don't you like it?'

I nodded.

I had seen an almost identical one a few months ago, in the bicycle shop in Lucignano. But that one wasn't so nice, it didn't have a silvered tail-light and its front wheel wasn't small. I had gone in to look at it and the shop assistant, a tall man, with a moustache and a grey apron, had said, 'Smashing, isn't it?'

'Yes, it is.'

'Last one I've got. It's a bargain. Why don't you get your parents to buy it for you?

'I'd like to.'

'So what's the problem?'

'I've already got one.'

'That thing?' The shop assistant's lip had curled as he pointed at the Crock leaning against the lamp-post.

I justified myself: 'It used to be papa's.'

'It's time you changed it. Tell your parents. You'd look great on a beauty like this.'

I had gone away. I hadn't even bothered to ask him how much it cost.

This one was much nicer.

On the top of the crossbar were the English words Red Dragon, in gold letters.

'What does Red Dragon mean?' I asked papa.

He shrugged and said: 'Your mother knows.'

Mama covered her mouth and giggled. 'Idiot! Since when did I know any English?'

Papa looked at me. 'Well, what are you waiting for? Aren't you going to try it out?'

'Now?'

'When else, tomorrow?'

I felt embarrassed about trying it out in front of everyone. 'Can I take it indoors?'

Skull got on it. 'If you don't try it out, I will.'

Mama cuffed him round the ear. 'Get off that bicycle this minute! It's Michele's.'

'You really want to take it upstairs?' papa asked me.

'Yes.'

'Can you carry it?'

'Yes.'

'All right, but just for today…'

'Are you crazy, Pino?' Mama said. 'A bicycle in the house? It'll leave tyremarks.'

'He'll be careful.'

My sister took off her glasses, threw them on the ground and burst into tears.

'Maria, pick up those glasses at once,' papa barked.

She crossed her arms. 'No! I won't, it's not fair. All for Michele and nothing for me!'

'You wait your turn.' Papa took out of the truck a package wrapped in blue paper and tied up with a bow.

'This is for you.'

Maria put her glasses back on. She tried to undo the knot but couldn't, so she tore at it with her teeth.

'Wait! It's nice paper, we'll keep it.' Mama undid the bow and took off the paper.

Inside was a Barbie with a crown on her head and a tight-fitting white satin dress and bare arms.

Maria nearly fainted. 'The dancer Barbie...!' She flopped against me. 'She's beautiful.'

Papa closed the tarpaulin of the truck. 'That's it. No more presents for the next ten years.'

Maria and I went up the front steps. She with her dancer Barbie in her hand, I with the bicycle on my back.

'Isn't she beautiful?' said Maria looking at the doll.

'Yes she is. What are you going to call her?'

'Barbara.'

'Why Barbara?'

'Because Barbara said that when she grows up she'll be like Barbie. And Barbie's English for Barbara.'

'And what are you going to do with Poor Poppet, throw her away?'

'No. She can be the maid.' Then she looked at me. 'Didn't you like your present?' she asked.

'Yes. But I thought it would be something else.'

That night I slept with the old man.

I had just got into bed and was finishing *Tex* when he came into the bedroom. He looked as if another twenty years had been dumped on him. His face was so gaunt it had shrunk to a skeleton.

'You asleep?' he yawned.

I closed the comic and turned towards the wall. 'No.'

'Ahhh! I'm shattered.' He switched on the bedside lamp and started getting undressed. 'What with the journey there and the journey back, God knows how many kilometres I've done. My back's killing me. I need some sleep.' He held his trousers up in the air, inspected them and made a wry face. 'I'm going to have to get some new clothes.' He took off his half-boots and socks and put them on the windowsill.

His feet smelled.

He rummaged in his suitcase, got out the bottle of Stock 84 and took a swig from it. He grimaced and wiped his mouth with his hand. 'Ugh, what muck.' He picked up the folder, opened it, looked at the pack of photographs and asked me, 'Do you want to see my son?' He passed me a photo.

It was the one I had seen the morning I had gone through his things. Francesco dressed as a mechanic.

'Handsome lad, isn't he?'

'Yes, he is.'

'Here he was still well, later he lost weight.'

A brown moth came in through the window and started knocking against the lampshade. It made a dull thud every time it hit the incandescent glass.

The old man picked up a newspaper and squashed it against the wall. 'Fucking moths.' He passed me another photo. 'My home.'

It was a low cottage with red windows. Behind the thatched roof you could see the tops of four palm trees. Sitting in the doorway was a black girl in a yellow bikini. She had long hair and was holding a joint of ham in her hands, like a trophy. Next to the house there was a small square garage and in front of it a huge white car with no roof and black windows.

'What kind of car's that?' I asked.

'A Cadillac. I bought it second-hand. It's in perfect condition. All I had to do was change the tyres.' He took off his shirt. 'It was a bargain.'

'And who's that black girl?'

He lay down on the bed. 'My wife.'

'You've got a black wife?'

'Yes. I left my old one. This one's twenty-three years old. Little doll. Sonia, her name is. And if you think that's ham, you're wrong, it's speck. Genuine Venetian. I brought it to her all the way from Italy. You can't get it in Brazil, it's a delicacy. It was a real hassle carrying it. They even stopped me at customs. Wanted to cut it open, thought there were drugs inside…Ah well, I'm going to put out the light, I'm tired.'

Darkness fell in the room. I could hear him breathing and making funny noises with his mouth.

After a while he said, 'You can't imagine what it's like over there. Everything's dirt cheap. Everybody serving you. You don't do shit all day. Beats this fucking country any day. I've finished with this country.'

'Where *is* Brazil?' I asked him.

'Far away. Too far. Good night and sweet dreams.'

'Good night.'

AND EVERYTHING stopped.

A fairy had put Acqua Traverse to sleep. The days followed one another, scorching, identical and endless.

The grown-ups didn't even go out in the evenings. Before, after dinner, they had put out the tables and played cards. Now they stayed indoors. Felice wasn't around any more. Papa stayed in bed all day and only talked to the old man. Mama cooked. Salvatore had shut himself up at home.

I rode my new bike. Everyone wanted a go on it. Skull could get right through Acqua Traverse on one wheel. I couldn't even get two metres.

I often went out on my own. I cycled along the dried-up stream, I rode down dusty little tracks between the fields that took me far away, where there was nothing but fallen posts and rusty barbed wire. Away in the distance the red combine harvesters shimmered in the waves of heat that rose from the fields.

It was as if God had given the whole world a haircut.

Sometimes the trucks with the sacks of wheat passed through Acqua Traverse leaving trails of black smoke behind them.

When I was in the street I felt as if everyone was watching what I was doing. I thought I glimpsed, behind the windows, Barbara's mother spying on me, Skull pointing at me and whispering to Remo, Barbara smiling a strange smile at me. But even when I was alone, sitting on a branch of the carob or on my bike, that feeling didn't leave me. Even when I forced my way through the remains of that sea of wheat ears soon to be packed into bales and I had nothing but sky around me, I felt as if a thousand eyes were watching me.

I won't go there, don't worry, everybody. I've sworn I won't.

But the hill was there, and it was waiting for me.

I started to ride along the road that led to Melichetti's farm. And every day, without realising it, I went a bit further.

Filippo had forgotten about me. I felt it.

I tried to call him with my thoughts.

Filippo? Filippo, can you hear me?

I can't come. I can't.

He wasn't thinking about me.

Maybe he was dead. Maybe he wasn't there any more.

One afternoon, after lunch, I lay down on my bed to read. The light pressed against the shutters and filtered into the boiling room. I had the crickets in my ears. I fell asleep with the *Tiramolla* comic in my hand.

I dreamed that it was night but I could still see. The hills were shifting in the dark. They moved slowly like tortoises under a carpet. Then all together they opened their eyes, red holes that gaped in the wheat, and they rose up, sure that no one could see them, and became earthy, wheat-covered giants that undulated across the fields and rolled over me and buried me.

I woke up bathed in sweat. I went to the fridge to get some water. I could see the giants.

I went out and got the Crock.

I was at the end of the path that led to the abandoned house.

The hill was there. Hazy, veiled by the heat. I thought I could see two black eyes in the wheat, just below the summit, but they were only patches of light, folds in the ground. The sun had started to sink and weaken. The hill's shadow slowly covered the plain.

I could go up.

But papa's voice held me back. 'Listen to me carefully. If you go back there they'll kill him. They've sworn it.'

Who? Who had sworn it? Who would kill him?

The old man? No. Not him. He wasn't strong enough.

Them, the earth giants. The lords of the hill. Now they were lying in the fields and were invisible, but at night they woke up and crossed the countryside. If I now went to see Filippo, even though it was daytime, they would rise up like waves of the ocean and reach there and dump their earth in the hole and bury him.

Turn back, Michele. Turn back, my sister's shrill little voice told me.

I veered my bike round and launched myself into the wheat, among the holes, pedalling like a madman and hoping I'd ride over the backbone of one of those damned monsters.

I was hiding under a rock in the dried-up stream.

I was sweating. The flies wouldn't leave me alone.

Skull had flushed them all out. I was the only one left. Now it was getting difficult. I would have to dash out, without stopping, cut across the field of stubble, reach the carob and shout, 'Den free everybody!'

But Skull was there, near the tree, pointing like a hound, and when he saw me running he would rush out himself and in a few strides he would catch me.

I'd have to run and hope for the best, if I made it, fine, if I didn't, too bad.

I was just about to set off, when a black shadow swooped down on me.

Skull!

It was Salvatore. 'Move over, or he'll see me. He's close by.'

I made room for him and he got under the rock too.

Without wanting to, I blurted out, 'What about the others?'

'He's caught them all. Only you and me are left.'

It was the first time we had spoken to each other since that day with Felice.

Skull had asked me why I had quarrelled with him.

'We haven't quarrelled. It's just that I don't like Salvatore,' I had replied.

Skull had put his arm round my shoulders. 'Good for you. He's a shit.'

Salvatore dried the sweat from his forehead.

'Who's going to make den?'

'You go.'

'Why?'

'Because you're faster.'

'I can run faster over a long distance, but you're quicker to the carob.'

I said nothing.

'I've got an idea,' he went on. 'Let's go out together, both of us. When Skull comes I'll get in his way and you run to the carob. That way we'll beat him. What do you say?'

'It's a good idea. Except that I'll make den and you'll lose.'

'It doesn't matter. It's the only way to fuck that pea-brain.'

I smiled.

He looked at me and stretched out his hand.

'Peace?'

'All right.' I grasped it.

'Did you know Signora Destani isn't taking our class any more? A new teacher's coming this year.'

'Who told you?'

'My aunt talked to the head. She says she's beautiful. And maybe she doesn't whack like Destani.'

I tore up a tuft of grass. 'It makes no difference to me anyway.'

'Why not?'

'Because we're leaving Acqua Traverse.'

Salvatore looked at me in surprise. 'Where are you going?'

'To the North.'

'Whereabouts?'

I said the first name that came into my head. 'Pavia.'

'Where's Pavia?'

I shrugged. 'I don't know. But we're going to live in a palazzo, on the top floor. And papa's going to buy a 131 Mirafiori. And I'm going to go to school there.'

Salvatore picked up a stone and tossed it from one hand to the other. 'And you'll never come back again?'

'No.'

'And you won't see the schoolmistress?'

I looked at the ground. 'No.'

'I'm sorry,' he whispered. He looked at me. 'Ready?'

'Ready.'

'Let's go, then. And don't stop. On the count of three.'

'One, two, three,' and we sprinted off.

'There they are! There they are!' Remo shouted, from his perch in the carob.

But there was nothing Skull could do, we were too quick. We banged into the carob together and shrieked, 'Den free everybody!'

WE HAD woken up and everything was veiled with grey. It was cold, it was damp, and sudden gusts of wind shifted the sultry air. In the night some large restless clouds had piled up on the horizon and started to advance on Acqua Traverse.

We watched them spellbound. We had forgotten that water could fall from the sky.

Now we were under the shed. I was stretched out on the sacks of wheat, with my head in my hands, quite relaxed, watching the wasps build a nest. The others had sat down in a circle by the plough. Salvatore was lounging on the iron seat of the tractor, with his feet on the steering wheel.

I loved those wasps. Remo had knocked their house down at least ten times by throwing stones at it, but those stubborn little creatures always came back to rebuild it in the same spot, at the meeting point of two metal posts and a gutter. They stuck the straw and wood together with their saliva and built a nest that looked as if it was made of cardboard.

The others were chatting, but I wasn't paying attention.

Skull as usual was talking in a loud voice and Salvatore was listening in silence.

I wished it would start raining, everyone was fed up with the drought.

I heard Barbara say, 'Why don't we go to Lucignano and have an ice-cream? I've got the money.'

'Have you got the money for us, too?'

'No. It's not enough. Might be enough for two tubs.'

'What are we supposed to do in Lucignano, then? Watch you stuffing yourself with ice-cream and getting even fatter?'

Why did those wasps make the nest? Who had taught them to do it?

'They just know. It's in their nature,' papa had replied once when I had asked him.

My sister came over to me and said, 'I'm going home. What are you going to do?'

'I'm staying here.'

'All right. I'm going to make myself some bread and butter and sugar. Bye.' She went off followed by Togo.

And what was in my nature? What could I do?

'Well?' asked Remo. 'What about a game of steal-the-flag?'

I could climb the carob. I was very good at that and nobody had taught me how to do it.

Skull got up, kicked the ball and sent it across to the other side of the road.

'Hey, I've got a great idea. Why don't we go where we went that time?'

Maybe I could go and join Maria and make myself a slice of bread and butter and sugar as well, but I wasn't hungry.

'Where?'

'Up on the mountain.'

'What mountain?'

'To the abandoned house. Near Melichetti's farm.'

I turned. My body suddenly awoke, my heart started marching in my chest and my stomach tightened.

Barbara wasn't convinced. 'What do you want to go there for? It's a long way. And what if it starts raining?'

Skull mimicked her. 'And what if it starts raining? We'll get wet! Nobody asked you to come anyway.'

Remo didn't seem very keen either. 'What could we do there?'

'Explore the house. Last time only Michele went in.'

Remo said something to me.

I looked at him. 'Sorry? I didn't catch that.'

'What's inside the house?' he asked me.

'Eh?'

'What's inside the house?'

I couldn't speak, I had no saliva. I stammered. 'Nothing…I don't know…' I felt as if an icy liquid was running down from my head, into my neck and down my sides. 'Some old furniture, a cooker, that sort of thing.'

Skull asked Salvatore, 'Shall we go?'

'No, I don't feel like it,' Salvatore shook his head. 'Barbara's right, it's a long way.'

'I'm going. We can make it our secret base.' Skull got his bike, which was leaning against the tractor. 'Anyone who wants to come, come. Anyone who doesn't want to come, don't come.' He asked Remo, 'What are you going to do?'

'I'll come.' Remo got up and asked Barbara, 'Are you coming?'

'As long as there are no races.'

'No races,' Skull assured her and asked Salvatore again. 'Aren't you coming then?'

I waited, without saying anything.

'I'll do whatever Michele does,' said Salvatore and, looking me in the eyes, he asked, 'Well, are you going?'

I got to my feet and said, 'Yes, I'll go.'

Salvatore jumped down from the tractor. 'Right, let's go then.'

We were cycling, all of us, just like the first time, towards the hill.

We rode in single file. Only my sister was missing.

The atmosphere was close and the sky was an unnatural scarlet colour. The clouds, previously massed on the horizon, were now gathering above us and jostling each other like hordes of Huns before a battle. They were large and sombre. The sun was opaque and turbid as if a filter was screening it. The air was neither hot nor cold, but it was windy. At the sides of the road and on the fields the hay was packed up in bales, which were arranged like pawns on a chessboard. Where the combine harvester hadn't passed, long waves formed, ruffling the wheat.

Remo eyed the horizon anxiously. 'It's going to rain any moment.'

The closer I got to the hill the worse I felt. A weight pressed on my stomach. The remains of breakfast rolled around in my stomach. I felt breathless and a veil of sweat bathed my back and my neck.

What was I doing? Every turn of the pedal was a

piece of oath crumbling away.

'Listen to me, Michele, you mustn't go back there ever again. If you go back they'll kill him. And it'll be your fault.'

'I won't go back there again.'

'Swear it on my head.'

'I swear.'

'Say, I swear on your head that I won't go back there again.'

'I swear on your head that I won't go back there again.'

I was breaking the oath, I was going to see Filippo and if they found me they would kill him.

I wanted to turn back, but my legs pedalled and an irresistible force dragged me towards the hill.

A distant rumble of thunder ripped the silence.

'Let's go home,' said Barbara as if she had heard my thoughts.

'Yes,' I panted, 'let's go home.'

Skull passed us guffawing. 'If a few drops of rain scare the shit out of you, you better had go home.'

Barbara and I looked at each other and kept pedalling.

The wind increased. It blew on the fields and raised the chaff in the air. It was hard to keep the bikes on line, the gusts drove us off the road.

'Here we are. A long way, was it?' said Skull, braking to make his wheels skid on the grit.

The path leading to the house was there in front of us.

Salvatore looked at me and asked, 'Shall we go?'

'Yes, let's go.'

We started the climb. I had trouble keeping up with the others. Red Dragon was a rip-off. I didn't want to admit it, but it was. If you stood up on the pedals you got the handlebars in your mouth and if you changed gear the chain came off. The only way to avoid being left behind was to stay in top gear.

From the fields, on our right, a flock of rooks rose. They cawed and wheeled with outspread wings, borne on the air currents.

The sun was swallowed up by the grey and suddenly it seemed like evening. A clap of thunder. Another. I looked at the clouds as they rolled and wrapped over each other. Now and then one of them lit up as if a firework had exploded inside it.

The thunderstorm was coming.

What if Filippo was dead?

A white corpse huddled at the bottom of a hole. Covered with flies and swollen with grubs and worms, its hands withered and its lips hard and grey.

No, he wasn't dead.

What if he didn't recognise me? If he wouldn't speak to me any more?

'Filippo, it's Michele. I've come back. I swore to you I would, I've come back.'

'You're not Michele. Michele's dead. And he lives in a hole like me. Go away.'

In front of us the valley opened up. It was sombre and silent. The birds and the crickets were mute.

When we arrived at the oaks a big heavy drop hit my forehead, another my arm and another my shoulder and the storm broke over us. The rain teemed down. The downpour lashed the tree-tops and the wind blew among the branches, whistled among the leaves, and the earth sucked up the water like a dry sponge and the drops rebounded on the hard earth and vanished and the lightning struck on the fields.

'We'd better get some shelter!' shouted Skull. 'Run!'

We ran, but we were already drenched. I slowed down. If I saw the 127 or anything strange I was going to leg it.

There were no cars around and I couldn't see anything strange.

They went into the cowshed. The hole was there, behind the brambles. I wanted to run and uncover it and see Filippo, but I forced myself to follow them.

The others were standing there, jumping up and down, excited by the thunderstorm. We took off our T-shirts and wrung them out. Barbara had to pull hers forward, otherwise her tits would have shown.

Everyone was laughing nervously and rubbing cold arms and looking outside. It was as if the sky had been riddled with holes. As the thunder crashed the lightning joined the clouds to the earth. The clearing, in a few minutes, filled with puddles and from the sides of the valley dirty streams of red earth flowed down.

Filippo must be scared to death. All that water was draining into the hole and if it didn't stop soon it might drown him. The sound of the rain on the corrugated sheet was deafening him.

I must go to him.

'Upstairs there's a motorbike,' I heard my voice saying.

They all turned to look at me.

'Yes, there's a motorbike…'

Skull jumped to his feet as if he had sat on an ants' nest. 'A motorbike?'

'Yes.'

'Where is it?'

'Upstairs. In the last room.'

'What's it doing there?'

I shrugged. 'I don't know.'

'Do you reckon it still works?'

'It might.'

Salvatore looked at me, he had a mocking smile on his face. 'Why did you never tell us?'

Skull cocked his head. 'Right! Why did you never tell us, eh?'

I swallowed. 'Because I didn't want to. I'd done the forfeit.'

A flash of understanding went through his eyes. 'Let's go and have a look at it. Wow, if it works…'

Skull, Salvatore and Remo rushed out of the cowshed, sheltering their heads with their hands and shoving each other into the puddles.

Barbara set off, but stopped in the rain. 'Aren't you coming?'

'In a minute. You go on.'

The water had slicked her hair which hung down like dirty spaghetti. 'Don't you want me to wait for you?'

'No, you go on. I won't be a minute.'

'All right.' She ran off.

I went round the house and made my way through the brambles. My heart was beating in my eardrums and my legs were giving at the knees. I reached the clearing. It had turned into a rain-lashed bog.

The hole was open.

The green fibreglass sheet wasn't there any more, neither was the mattress.

The water was dripping down me, trickling inside my shorts and pants, and my hair clung to my forehead and the hole was there, a black mouth in the dark earth, and I went towards it. I was hardly breathing, I clenched my fists, while around me the sky was falling and waves of incandescent pain wrapped round my throat.

I closed my eyes and opened them again hoping something would change.

The hole was still there. Black as the plughole in a sink.

I staggered closer. My feet in the mud. I wiped one hand across my face to dry it. I was almost collapsing on the ground, but I kept going forward.

He's not there. Don't look. Go away.

I stopped.

Go on. Go and look.

I can't.

I looked at my sandals covered in muck. Take one step, I told myself. I did. Take another. I did. Good boy. Another and then another. And I saw the edge of the hole in front of my feet.

You're there.

Now all I had to do was look into it.

I suddenly felt certain there was nobody in there any more.

I raised my head and looked.

I was right. There was nothing there. Not even the bucket and the little saucepan. Only dirty water and a sodden blanket.

They had taken him away. Without telling me anything. Without letting me know.

He had gone away and I hadn't even said goodbye.

Where was he? I didn't know, but I knew that he was mine and that they had taken him away from me.

'Where are you?' I shouted into the rain.

I fell on my knees. I dug my fingers in the mud and squeezed it in my hands.

'There isn't any motorbike.'

I turned round.

Salvatore.

He was standing there. A few metres away from me, his T-shirt soaked, his trousers spattered with mud. 'There isn't any motorbike, is there?'

I gurgled no.

He pointed towards the hole. 'Is that where he was?'

I nodded, and stammered, 'They've taken him away.'

Salvatore came over, looked inside and stared at me. 'I know where he is.'

I slowly raised my head. 'Where is he?'

'He's at Melichetti's. Down in the gravina.'

'How do you know?'

'I heard yesterday. Papa was talking to your father and that guy from Rome. I hid behind the study door and heard them. They moved him. The exchange didn't work out, they said.' He swept back his wet fringe. 'They said this place wasn't safe any more.'

The thunderstorm passed.

Quickly, just as it had started.

It was a long way off now. A dark mass advancing over the countryside, drenching it and continuing on its way.

We were going down the path.

The air was so clean that far away, beyond the ochre plain, you could see a thin green strip. The sea. It was the first time I had ever seen it from Acqua Traverse.

The downpour had left a smell of wet grass and earth and a slight coolness. The clouds left in the sky were white and frayed and blades of dazzling sun cut the plain. The birds had started chirping again, it sounded like a singing contest.

I had told Skull it had been a practical joke.

'Ha ha, bloody hilarious,' he had replied.

I had a presentiment that no one would go up on that hill again, it was too far away, and there was nothing interesting about that old ruin. And that hidden valley brought bad luck.

Filippo had ended up at Melichetti's with the pigs, because the exchange hadn't worked out and because the hole wasn't safe any more, that's what they had said. And the lords of the hill and the monsters I invented had nothing to do with it.

'Stop all this talk about monsters, Michele. Monsters don't exist. It's men you should be afraid of, not monsters.' That's what papa had said to me.

It was his fault. He hadn't let him go and he never would let him go.

Cats, when they catch lizards, play with them, they play with them even if the lizard is all open and its innards are hanging out and it has lost its tail. They follow it calmly, they sit down and knock it and amuse themselves till the lizard dies, and when it's dead they hardly touch it with their paw, as if it disgusted them, and the lizard doesn't move any more and then they look at it and they go away.

A deafening roar, a metallic din shattered the calm and swamped everything.

Barbara shouted, pointing at the sky, 'Look! Look!'

From behind the hill two helicopters appeared. Two iron dragonflies, two big blue dragonflies with 'Carabinieri' written on the sides.

They dipped down over us and we started waving our arms and shouting, they came alongside, and turned at the same time, as if they wanted to show us how clever they were, then they skimmed across the fields, flew over Acqua Traverse and disappeared on the horizon.

The grown-ups had gone.

The cars were there, but they weren't.

The houses empty, the doors open.

We all ran from one house to another.

Barbara was agitated. 'Is there anyone at your house?'

'No. What about yours?'

'There's nobody there either.'

'Where are they?' Remo was out of breath. 'I've even looked in the vegetable garden.'

'What shall we do?' asked Barbara.

'I don't know,' I replied.

Skull was walking along the middle of the road, with his hands in his pockets and a grim face, like a gunfighter in a ghost town. 'Who cares. Good riddance. I've been longing for the day when they'd all just fuck off.' And he spat.

'Michele!'

I turned round.

My sister was in vest and knickers, outside the shed, with her Barbies in her hands and Togo following her like a shadow.

I ran over to her. 'Maria! Maria! Where are the grown-ups?'

She answered calmly, 'At Salvatore's house.'

'Why?'

She pointed at the sky. 'The helicopters.'

'What?'

'That's why, the helicopters went over, and afterwards they all came out in the street and they were shouting and they went to Salvatore's house.'

'Why?'

'I don't know.'

I looked around. Salvatore wasn't there any more.

'And what are you doing here?'

'Mama told me I've got to wait here. She asked me where you'd gone.'

'And what did you tell her?'

'I told her you'd gone on the mountain.'

The grown-ups stayed at Salvatore's house all evening.

We waited in the courtyard, sitting on the edge of the fountain.

'When are they going to finish?' Maria asked me for the hundredth time.

And I for the hundredth time answered: 'I don't know.'

They had told us to wait, they were talking.

Barbara went up the steps and knocked on the door every five minutes, but nobody came. She was worried.

'What are they talking about all this time?'

'I don't know.'

Skull had gone off with Remo. Salvatore was indoors, doubtless hiding away in his room.

Barbara sat down beside me. 'What on earth's going on?'

I shrugged.

She looked at me. 'What's the matter?'

'Nothing. I'm tired.'

'Barbara!' Angela Mura was at the window. 'Barbara, go home.'

Barbara asked, 'When are you coming?'

'Soon. Run along now.'

Barbara said goodbye to us and went off looking glum.

'When's my mama coming out?' Maria asked Angela Mura.

She looked at us and said, 'Go home and get your own supper, she'll be home soon.' She closed the window.

Maria shook her head. 'I'm not going, I'm waiting here.'

I got up. 'Come on, we'd better go.'

'No!'

'Come on. Give me your hand.'

She crossed her arms. 'No! I'll stay here all night, I don't care.'

'Give me your hand, come on.'

She straightened her glasses and got up. 'I won't sleep though.'

'Don't sleep then.'

And, hand in hand, we went home.

THEY WERE shouting so loud they woke us up.

We had grown used to all sorts of things. Nocturnal meetings, noise, raised voices, broken plates, but now they were shouting too much.

'Why are they screaming like that?' Maria asked me, lying on her bed.

'I don't know.'

'What time is it?'

'Late.'

It was the middle of the night, the room was dark and we were in our bedroom, wide awake.

'Make them stop,' Maria complained. 'They're disturbing me. Tell them to scream more quietly.'

'I can't.'

I tried to understand what they were saying, but the voices mingled together.

Maria lay down beside me. 'I'm scared.'

'They're scared.'

'Why?'

'Because they're shouting.'

Those shouts were like the spitting of the green lizards.

Green lizards, when they can't get away and you're about to catch them, open their mouths, swell up and spit and try to scare you because they're more scared of you, you're the giant, and all they can do is try and frighten you. And if you don't know that they're harmless, that they don't hurt, that it's all a sham, you don't touch them.

The door opened.

For an instant the room lit up. I saw the black figure of mama, and behind her the old man.

Mama closed the door. 'Are you awake?'

'Yes,' we replied.

She switched on the light on the bedside table. In her hand she had a plate with some bread and cheese. She sat on the edge of the bed. 'I've brought you something to eat.' She spoke quietly, with a tired voice. She had rings round her eyes, her hair was dishevelled and she looked worn. 'Eat up and go to sleep.'

'Mama…?' said Maria.

Mama put the plate on her knees. 'What is it?'

'What's going on?'

'Nothing.' Mama tried to cut the cheese, but her hand was shaking. She wasn't a good actress. 'Now eat up and…' She bent forward, laid the plate on the floor and put her hand to her face and began to cry silently.

'Mama…Mama…Why are you crying?' Maria started sobbing.

I felt a lump swelling in my throat too. I said, 'Mama? Mama?'

She raised her head and looked at me with glistening

red eyes. 'What is it?'

'He's dead, isn't he?'

She slapped me on the cheek and shook me as if I was made of cloth. 'Nobody's dead! Nobody's dead! Do you understand?' She gave a grimace of pain and whispered, 'You're too small…' She opened her mouth wide and clutched me to her breast.

I started to cry.

Now we were all crying.

In the other room the old man was shouting.

Mama heard him and pulled away from me. 'Stop it now!' She dried away her tears. She gave us two slices of bread. 'Eat up.'

Maria sank her teeth into the bread, but couldn't swallow for her sobs. Mama snatched the slice out of her hands.

'Aren't you hungry? It doesn't matter.' She picked up the plate. 'Lie down both of you.' She pulled away our pillows and put out the light. 'If the noises disturb you, put your heads under these. Here!' She put them on our heads.

I tried to get free. 'Mama, please. I can't breathe.'

'Do as you're told!' she snarled and pressed hard.

Maria was getting desperate, it sounded as if her throat was being cut.

'Stop it!' Mama shouted so loud that for an instant they even stopped quarrelling in the other room. I was scared she would hit her.

Maria went quiet.

If we moved, if we spoke, mama repeated like a cracked record, 'Shh! Go to sleep.'

I pretended to sleep and hoped Maria would do the

same. And after a while she settled down as well.

Mama stayed so long I was sure she was going to spend the whole night with us, but she got up. She thought we were asleep. She went out and shut the door.

We took off the pillows. It was dark, but the dim reflection of the streetlamp lightened the room. I got out of bed.

Maria sat up, put on her glasses and, sniffing, asked me, 'What are you doing?'

I put my finger to my nose. 'Quiet.'

I pressed my ear against the door.

They were still arguing, more softly now. I could hear Felice's voice and the old man's, but I couldn't make out what they were saying. I tried to look through the keyhole, but all I could see was the wall.

I grasped the handle.

Maria bit her hand. 'What are you doing, are you crazy?'

'Quiet!' I opened a crack.

Felice was on his feet, near the cooker. He was wearing a green tracksuit, the zip pulled down below his ribs showed his swollen pectorals. He was staring and his mouth was slightly open, showing his little milk teeth. He had shaven his head bare.

'Me?' he said putting a hand on his chest.

'Yes, you,' said the old man. He was sitting at the table, with one leg resting on the other knee, a cigarette between his fingers and a treacherous smile on his lips.

'Me a pansy? A poof?' Felice asked.

The old man confirmed this. 'Exactly.'

Felice cocked his head on one side. 'And…And how do you make that out?'

'It's written all over you. You're a poof. No doubt about

it. And…' The old man took a drag. 'You know what the worst thing is?'

Felice knitted his brow, interested. 'No, what is it?'

They sounded like two friends exchanging secret confidences.

The old man put out the stub in his plate. 'The worst thing is you don't know it. That's your problem. You were born a poof and you don't know it. You're a big boy now, you're not a kid any more. Come to terms with it. You'd feel better. You'd do what poofs do, take it up the arse. Instead you act tough, play the man, shoot your mouth off, but everything you do and say sounds fake, sounds poof-like.'

Papa was standing up and seemed to be following the conversation, but he was on the other side of the room. The barber was leaning against the door as if the house was likely to fall down at any moment and mama, sitting on the sofa, with a vacant expression on her face, was watching the television with the sound turned off. The lampshade was enveloped in a cloud of midges that fell down black and stiff on the white plates.

'Listen all of you, listen, let's give him back to her. Let's give him back to her,' papa said suddenly.

The old man looked at him, shook his head and smiled. 'You'll keep quiet if you know what's good for you.'

Felice glanced at papa, then went over to the old man. 'Reckon I'm a poof, do you, you piece of Roman shit? Well you can have this fistful from me.' He brought his arm up and punched him in the mouth.

The old man crashed to the floor.

I took two steps backwards and clutched my head in my hands. Felice had hit the old man. I started shaking and my gorge rose, but I couldn't help looking again.

In the kitchen papa was shouting. 'What the hell are you doing? Are you out of your mind?' He had grabbed Felice by one arm and tried to pull him away.

'He called me a poof, the bastard…' Felice was almost blubbing. 'I'll kill him…'

The old man was on the ground. I felt sorry for him. I wanted to help him but I couldn't. He tried to get up again, but his feet slipped on the floor and his arms wouldn't support him. Blood and saliva were dripping from his mouth. The glasses he wore on his head were now under the table. I kept looking at those thin, white, hairless calves that emerged from his blue cotton trousers. He clutched the edge of the table and slowly pulled himself up onto his feet. He picked up a napkin and pressed it to his mouth.

Mama was crying on the sofa. The barber was flat against the door as if he had seen the devil.

Felice took two steps towards the old man even though papa tried to hold him back. 'Well? Did that feel like a poof's punch, then? Call me a poof one more time and I swear you'll never get up again.'

The old man sat on a chair and with his napkin stanched an enormous split in his lip. Then he raised his head and stared at Felice and said in a steady voice, 'If you're a man, prove it.' An evil light flashed in his eyes. 'You said you'd do it and you chickened out. What was it you said? Slit him open like a lamb, I will, no problem, I'm not scared. I'm a paratrooper. I'm this, I'm that. Loudmouth, you're nothing but a loudmouth. You're worse than a dog, can't even keep guard over a kid.' He spat a mouthful of blood on the table.

'You piece of shit!' Felice whimpered, dragging papa

along behind him. 'I'm not doing it! Why should *I* have to do it, why?' Two trickles of tears ran down his shaven cheeks.

'Help me! Help me!' papa shouted to Barbara's father. And the barber threw himself on Felice. The two of them together could barely hold him.

'I'm not doing it, you bastard!' Felice repeated. 'I'm not doing time for you. Forget it!'

He's going to kill him, I said to myself.

The old man got to his feet. 'I'll do it, then. But don't you worry, if I go down, you go down. I'll take you down with me, you arsehole. You can be sure of that.'

'Take me down where, you Roman shit?' Felice drove forward, head down. Papa and the barber tried to restrain him but he shook them off like dandruff and charged at the old man again.

The old man took his pistol out of his trousers and put it against Felice's forehead. 'Try and hit me again. Try it. Do it, go on. Please, do it…'

Felice froze as if he was playing one-two-three-star.

Papa got between them. 'Calm down, for Christ's sake! You're a pain in the arse, the pair of you!' And he separated them.

'Try it!' The old man stuck the pistol in his belt. On Felice's forehead there was still a little red circle.

Mama, sitting in a corner, was crying and repeating with her hand over her mouth, 'Quiet! Be quiet! Be quiet! Be quiet!'

'Why does he want to shoot him?'

I turned round.

Maria had got up and was standing behind me.

'Go back to bed,' I shouted at her in a whisper.

She shook her head.

'Maria, go back to bed!'

My sister pursed her lips and shook her head.

I raised my hand, I was about to give her a cuff, but I restrained myself. 'Go back to bed and don't you dare cry.'

She obeyed.

Papa in the meantime had managed to get them to sit down. But he himself kept walking to and fro, with glistening eyes. A mad gleam had ignited in them.

'Right. Let's take a count. How many of us are there? Four. In the end, of all that number we started out with, there are just four of us left. The dumbest ones. Well, all the better. The loser kills him. It's so easy.'

'And gets life,' said the barber putting his hand on his forehead.

'Good man!' The old man clapped his hands. 'I see we're beginning to use our heads.'

Papa picked up a box of matches and showed it around. 'Right. Let's play a game. Do you know the soldier's draw?'

I shut the door.

I knew that game.

In the dark I found my T-shirt and trousers and put them on. Where had my sandals got to?

Maria was on her bed watching me. 'What are you doing?'

'Nothing.' They were in a corner.

'Where are you going?'

I put them on. 'Somewhere.'

'You know something, you're nasty, really nasty.'

I got onto the bed and from there onto the windowsill.

'What are you doing?'

I looked down. 'I'm going to see Filippo.' Papa had parked the Lupetto under our window, luckily.

'Who's Filippo?'

'He's a friend of mine.'

It was a long way down and the tarpaulin was rotten. Papa was always saying he must buy a new one. If I fell on it feet first it would tear and I would crash down onto the floor of the truck.

'If you do that I'll tell mama.'

I looked at her. 'Don't worry. The truck's there. You go to sleep. If mama comes…' What was she to tell her? 'Tell her…Tell her anything you like.'

'But she'll be cross.'

'It doesn't matter.' I crossed myself, held my breath, stepped forward and let myself fall open-armed.

I landed on my back in the middle of the tarpaulin completely unscathed. It held.

Maria put her head out of the window. 'Come back soon, please.'

'I won't be long. Don't worry.' I climbed onto the driver's cabin and from there got down to the ground.

The street was gloomy, like that starless night. The only lighted windows were the ones in my house. The street-lamp by the drinking fountain was surrounded by a ball of midges.

The sky was overcast again and Acqua Traverse was wrapped in a thick black mantle of darkness. I would have to enter it to get to Melichetti's farm.

I must be brave.

Tiger Jack. Think of Tiger Jack.

The Indian would help me. Before making any move, I must think what the Indian would do in my place. That was the secret.

I ran round to the back of the house to get my bike. My heart was already hammering at my chest.

Red Dragon, bold and brightly coloured, was resting on top of the Crock.

I was on the point of taking it, but I said to myself, am I crazy? How far am I going to get on that stupid contraption?

I was flying along on the old Crock.

I urged myself on. 'Go, Tiger, go.'

I was immersed in ink. I could hardly see the road and when I couldn't see it I imagined it. Now and then the feeble glow of the moon managed to seep through the quilt of clouds that covered the sky and then I glimpsed for a few moments the fields and the black silhouettes of the hills on either side of the track.

I gritted my teeth and counted the turns of the pedal.

One, two, three, breath…

One, two, three, breath…

The tyres crackled on the grit. The wind stuck to my face like a warm cloth.

The screech of a little owl, the bark of a distant dog. There was silence. But I could still hear their whispers in the darkness.

I imagined them at each side of the road, little

creatures, with foxes' ears and red eyes, watching me and talking among themselves.

'Look! Look, a boy!'

'What's he doing here at night?'

'Let's get him!'

'Yes, yes, yes, he looks tasty…Let's get him!'

And behind me were the lords of the hills, the earthy wheat-covered giants following me, just waiting for me to go off the road so that they could roll over me and bury me. I could hear them breathing. They made the same noise as the wind in the wheat.

The secret was to keep in the middle of the road, but I must be ready for danger.

Lazarus wasn't scared of anything.

You'll see, I said to myself.

In the night Lazarus was luminous. He winked on and off like the sign outside the La Perla bar in Lucignano. And when he lit up you could see the ants crawling in his veins. He didn't move fast, I was sure of that, if he started running he would fall to pieces. The important thing was to go past him, without stopping, without slowing down.

'Filippo…I'm coming…Filippo…I'm coming…' I repeated, panting with the effort.

As I drew nearer to the farm a new, even more suffocating terror grew inside me. On the back of my head the hair stood up as straight as needles.

Melichetti's pigs.

The lords of the hills and all the other monsters terrified me, but I knew that they didn't exist, that I imagined them, that I couldn't talk about them to anyone else because they would have laughed at me, but the pigs I certainly could talk about because they really existed and they were hungry.

For living flesh.

'The dachshund tried to get away, but the pigs didn't give him a chance. Torn to shreds in two seconds.' That's what Skull had said.

Maybe Melichetti let them out at night. They prowled around the farm, huge and vicious, with sharp fangs and noses in the air.

The further I kept away from those brutes the better.

In the distance a dim light appeared in the gloom.

The farm.

I was almost there.

I braked. The wind had dropped. The air was still and calm. The sound of crickets came from the nearby gravina. I got off the bike and dumped it among the brambles, beside the road.

You couldn't see a thing.

I moved swiftly, hardly breathing, and kept looking over my shoulder. I was afraid the sharp claw of a monster would sink into my neck. Now I was on foot there were a lot of noises, rustles, bumps, strange sounds. All around me was a thick black mass that pressed against the road. I wet my dry lips, I had a bitter taste in my mouth. My heart was pounding in my throat.

I put the sole of my sandal on something slimy, I jumped, gave a muffled cry and fell over, grazing my knee.

'Who is it? Who is it?' I stammered and curled up in a ball, expecting to be enveloped by the squelchy stinging tentacles of a jellyfish.

Two dull thuds and a 'Bwaa bwaa bwaa.'

A toad! I had trodden on a wheatfield toad. The stupid

thing had been sitting in the middle of the road.

I got to my feet and limped on towards the dim light.

I hadn't even brought a torch. I could have taken the one in papa's truck.

When I reached the edge of the farmyard, I hid behind a tree.

The house was about a hundred metres away. The windows were dark. There was just a little lamp hanging beside the door, lighting up a bit of flaky wall and the rusty rocking chair.

Just beyond, in the darkness, were the pigsties. Even from there I could smell the revolting stench of their excrement.

Where could Filippo be?

Down in the gravina, Salvatore had said. I had been down in that long gully a couple of times in wintertime with papa, looking for mushrooms. It was all crags, holes and rock faces.

If I went across the fields I would come out on the edge of the gravina and from there I could get down to the bottom without having to go too near the house.

It was a good plan.

I ran across the fields. The wheat had been cut. In the daytime, without the crops, I would have been seen, but now, without the moon, I was safe.

I stopped at the top of the gorge. Below it was so black I couldn't make out how steep the rock was, whether it was smooth or whether there were footholds.

I kept cursing myself for not bringing the torch. I couldn't go down that way. I might get hurt.

The only thing for it was to get closer to the house. At that point the gravina was shallower, and there was a little track that went down between the rocks. But that was also where the pigs were.

I was covered in sweat.

'Pigs have a better sense of smell than any other animal, hounds are nothing like as good,' Skull's father, who was a hunter, used to say.

I couldn't go that way. They would smell me.

What would Tiger Jack do in my place?

He would face them. He would mow them down with his Winchester and make them into sausages to roast on the fire with Tex and Silver Hair.

No. That wasn't his style.

What would he do?

Think, I told myself. Try.

He would try to get the human smell off himself, that's what he would do.

The Indians, when they went buffalo hunting, smeared themselves with grease and put furs on their backs. That was what I must do: smear myself with earth. Not earth, shit. Much better. If I smelled of shit they wouldn't notice me.

I got as close as possible to the house, keeping in the dark.

The stink got worse.

As well as the crickets I could hear something else. Music. The sound of a piano and a hoarse voice singing: 'The water's icy cold, nobody will save me. I fell into the foaming brine while the dancers danced in line. Wave on wave...'

Was Melichetti a singer?

Someone was sitting on the rocking chair. On the ground, next to it, there was a radio. It was either Melichetti or his lame daughter.

201

I watched for a while, crouching behind the old tractor tyres.

The person looked dead.

I moved closer.

It was Melichetti.

His wizened head lolling on a filthy cushion, his mouth open and his double-barrelled shotgun on his knees. He was snoring so loud I could hear him from there.

The coast was clear.

I came out into the open, took a few steps and the shrill barks of a dog shattered the silence. For a moment the crickets stopped singing.

The dog! I had forgotten the dog.

Two red eyes ran in the darkness. He was pulling the chain behind him and emitting strangled barks.

I dived head first into the stubble.

'What is it? What's up? What's got into you?' Melichetti said with a start. He sat on the rocking chair and rotated his head like an owl. 'Tiberius! Quiet! Be quiet, Tiberius!'

But the brute just wouldn't stop barking, so Melichetti stretched, put on his orthopaedic collar and got up, turned off the radio and switched on his torch.

'Who's there? Who's there? Is anyone there?' he shouted into the darkness and made a couple of listless circuits of the farmyard with his shotgun under his arm, pointing the band of light around. He went back grumbling. 'Stop making that row. There's nobody there.'

The dog squashed down on the ground and started growling between his teeth.

Melichetti went into the house slamming the door.

I kept as far away as possible from the dog and

approached the pig enclosure. I could see, in the darkness, the square silhouettes of the sties. The pungent smell increased and burned my throat.

I must camouflage myself. I took off my T-shirt and shorts. Dressed only in pants I dipped my hands in the piss-soaked earth and screwing up my face I spread that foul muck over my chest, my arms, my legs and my face.

'Go, Tiger. Go and don't stop,' I whispered and started crawling forward on all fours. It was a struggle. My hands and knees sank into the mud.

The dog started barking again.

I found myself between two pigsties. In front of me was a passageway less than a metre wide that disappeared into the gloom.

I could hear them. They were there. They made deep low noises that resembled the roar of a lion. I could sense their strength in the darkness, they were moving in a herd and trampling with their trotters, and the bars shook under their shoves.

Keep going and don't turn round, I ordered myself.

I prayed that my armour of shit would work. If one of those beasts put its snout through the bars it could tear my leg off with one bite.

I could see the end of the pen when there was a sudden scuffling and some grunts, as if they were quarrelling.

I couldn't help looking.

A metre away, two vicious yellow eyes were watching me. Behind those little headlamps there must be hundreds of kilos of muscles, flesh and bristles and claws and fangs and hunger.

We stared at each other for an endless moment, then

the creature gave a sudden jerk and I was certain he was going to knock down the fence.

I shouted and jumped to my feet and ran and slipped in the dung and got up again, I started running again, open-mouthed, in the blackness, clenching my fists as tight as could be and suddenly I was in the air, I was flying, my heart was in my mouth and my guts closed in a fist of pain.

I had gone over the edge of the gravina.

I was plunging into the void.

I fell, a metre below, into the branches of an olive that grew out at an angle among the sheer rocks and spread its foliage over the drop.

I clung onto a branch. If that blessed tree hadn't been there to break my fall I would have been smashed to a pulp on the rocks. Like Francesco.

A segment of moon had opened a gap through the bluish clouds and I could see, below me, that long gash in the countryside.

I tried to turn round but the trunk was rocking like a bowsprit. Now it's going to break, I said to myself. I'll take the whole tree down with me.

My hands and legs were shaking and at every moment I felt I was going to slip down. When at last I gripped the rock between my fingers I breathed again. I climbed back up onto the edge of the gravina.

It was deep and stretched right and left for several hundred metres. Inside, it was all holes, gullies and trees.

Filippo could be anywhere.

To my right was the beginning of a path that wound steeply down between the white rocks. There was a pole fixed in the ground, and tied to it was a worn rope which

Melichetti evidently used to help him get down. I grabbed hold of it and went down the precipitous track. After a few metres I came to a terrace covered in dung. It was surrounded by a fence made of branches tied together. Some clothes, ropes and scythes were hanging on a projecting rock. A little further on there was a pile of wooden stakes. Three small goats and a larger one were tethered to a root that protruded from the earth. They stared at me.

I said to them, 'Don't just gawp at me like idiots, tell me where Filippo is.'

A silent black shadow dropped down on me from the sky, passed over me, I shielded my head with my hands.

A little owl.

It rose again, dissolved in the blackness, then swooped towards the terrace again and went back up into the sky.

Strange, they were friendly birds.

Why was it attacking me?

'I'm going, I'm going,' I whispered.

The track continued and I went on down holding the rope. I had to walk crouching down and feel with my hands the obstacles that appeared in front of me, as blind people do. When I reached the bottom of the gully I was astonished. The holly bushes, the thistles, the arbutuses, the moss and the rocks were covered with luminous dots that pulsed like tiny lighthouses in the night. Fireflies.

The clouds had thinned and a half-moon tinged the gravina with yellow. The crickets were singing. Melichetti's dog had stopped barking. There was peace.

In front of me was an olive grove and behind, on the other slope of the gully, a narrow cleft in the rock.

From inside there came an acid smell, of dung. I went in just a little way and heard movements and bleating. A carpet of sheep. They had been shut inside the cave with wire netting. They were crammed in like sardines. No room there for Filippo.

I went back to the other slope, but I couldn't find any holes, any dens to hide a boy in.

When I had jumped out of the window it hadn't even crossed my mind that I might not succeed in finding him. All I would have to do was go through the dark and not get eaten by the pigs and there he would be.

It wasn't like that.

The gravina was very long and they might have put Filippo somewhere else.

I was disheartened. 'Filippo, where are you?' I shouted. But very quietly. Melichetti might hear me. 'Answer me! Where are you? Answer me!'

Nothing.

Only a little owl replied. It made a strange noise, it seemed to be saying: 'All for me, all for me, all for me.' It might be the same one that had attacked me before.

It wasn't fair. I had come all that way, I had risked my life for him and he was nowhere to be found. I started running backwards and forwards between the rocks and the olives, at random, as desperation gripped me.

I felt so angry I seized a branch from the ground and started banging it against a rock, till my hands were sore. Then I sat down. I shook my head and tried to banish the thought that it had all been useless.

I had run away from home like a fool.

Papa must be furious. He would give me a thrashing.

They must have noticed I wasn't in my bedroom. And even if they hadn't, they would soon be arriving there to kill Filippo.

Papa and the old man in front, Felice and the barber behind. At top speed, in the dark, in the grey car with the gunsight on its bonnet, squashing the toads with its wheels.

Michele, what are you waiting for? Come home, Maria's voice ordered me.

'I'm coming,' I said.

I had done what I could and he had been impossible to find. It wasn't my fault.

I must move quickly, they could arrive at any moment.

If I ran, without stopping, I might get home before they went out. Nobody would have noticed anything. That would be good.

I climbed quickly among the rocks back up the path I had come down. Now there was a bit of light it was easier.

The little owl. It was wheeling above the terrace, and when it passed in front of the moon I could see its black silhouette, its short broad wings.

'What are you doing?' I ran across the terrace, near the goats, and the bird swooped again. I went on a little way and turned back to look at that crazy owl.

It kept wheeling over the terrace. It skimmed the heap of poles resting against the rock, wheeled round and returned, stubbornly.

Why was it behaving like that? Was there a mouse there? No. What, then?

Its nest!

Of course. Its nest. Its young.

Swallows, too, if you knock down their nest, keep

wheeling round and round till they die of exhaustion.

They had covered up the little owl's nest. And little owls make their nests in holes.

Holes!

I turned back and started shifting the piled-up stakes with the owl brushing past me. 'Wait, wait,' I said to her.

There was an opening in the rock, roughly concealed. An oval cleft as wide as the wheel of a truck.

The owl darted in.

It was pitch-black. And there was a smell of burnt wood and ash. I couldn't make out how deep it was.

I stuck my head in and called. 'Filippo?'

I was answered by the echo of my voice.

'Filippo?' I leaned further in. 'Filippo?'

I waited. Not a sound.

He wasn't there.

He isn't there. Run home, my sister's voice repeated.

I had taken three steps when I thought I heard a cry, a low moan.

Had I imagined it?

I turned back and put my head into the hole.

'Filippo? Filippo, are you there?'

And from the hole came 'Mmmm! Mmmm!'

'Filippo, is that you?'

'Mmmm!'

He was there!

I felt a weight dissolving in my chest, I leaned against the rock and slid down. I sat there, slumped on that terrace covered with goats' droppings, with a smile on my face.

I had found him.

I started crying. I dried my eyes with my hands.

'Mmmm!'

I got up. 'I'm coming. I won't be a moment. You see? I've come, I kept my promise. You see?'

A rope. I found one, coiled up near the scythes. I tied it to the root where the goats were and threw it into the hole. 'Here I come.'

I lowered myself down inside. My heart was pumping so hard that my chest and arms were shaking. The darkness made me giddy. I couldn't breathe. I felt as if I was swimming in petroleum and it was cold.

I hadn't even gone two metres when I touched the ground. It was covered with stakes, pieces of wood, piled-up crates of tomatoes. On all fours I groped in the dark with my hands. I was naked and shivering with cold.

'Filippo, where are you?'

'Mmmm!'

They had gagged him.

'I'm…' One foot got caught between the branches, I fell, with my arms forward, on top of some bundles of thorny twigs. A sharp pain bit my ankle. I cried out and a hot acid flood of bile came up to my throat. An icy wind swept my back and I felt as if my ears were on fire.

With shaking hands I pulled out my trapped foot. The pain pressed me inside my ankle. 'I think I've sprained my ankle,' I gasped. 'Where are you?'

'Mmmm!'

I dragged myself, with gritted teeth, towards the moan, and found him. He was under the bundles of wood. I took them off him and felt him. He was lying on the ground. Naked. His arms and legs were bound with packing tape.

'Mmmm!'

I put my hands on his face. He had tape over his mouth too.

'You can't talk. Wait, I'll take it off. It might hurt a bit.'

I tore it off. He didn't shout, but started to pant.

'How are you?'

He didn't say anything.

'Filippo, how are you? Answer me!'

He was panting like the hound that was bitten by the viper.

'Are you ill?'

I touched his chest. It was swelling and subsiding too quickly.

'Now we'll get out of here. We'll get out. Hang on a moment.'

I tried to untie his wrists and ankles. It was tight. Finally, with my teeth, desperately, I started to saw through the tape. I freed first his hands, then his feet.

'That's it. Let's go.' I took his arm. But the arm fell limply back. 'Get up, please. We must go, they're coming.' I tried to pull him up, but he fell back down like a puppet. There wasn't a scrap of energy left in that exhausted little body. The only difference between him and a corpse was that he was still breathing. 'I can't carry you up. My leg hurts! Please, Filippo, help me…' I grasped him by the arms. 'Come on! Come on!' I sat him up, but as soon as I let go he flopped down on the ground. 'What have I got to do? Don't you recognise they'll shoot you if you stay here?' A lump blocked up my throat. 'Die like this then, you fool, you stupid fool! I came here for your sake, all the way here, I kept my promise and you…and you…' I burst into tears. I was shaken by my sobs. 'You…must…get…up…idiot,

idiot…you…idiot.' I tried again and again, stubbornly, but he sprawled back in the ashes, with his head all bent, like a dead chicken. 'Get up! Get up!' I shouted, and I pummelled him.

I didn't know what to do. I sat down, with my head on my knees. 'You're not dead yet, do you understand?' I sat there, crying. "This isn't heaven.'

For an instant he stopped panting and whispered something.

I put my ear to his lips. 'What did you say?'

He whispered, 'I can't do it.'

I shook him. 'What do you mean you can't do it?'

'I can't do it, I'm sorry.'

'Yes you can. Yes…'

He wasn't speaking any more. I embraced him. Covered in mud, we were shivering with cold. There was nothing more to be done. I couldn't do it either. I felt tired out, dead beat, my ankle was still throbbing. I shut my eyes, my heart started to relax and without wanting to I fell asleep.

I opened my eyes again.

It was dark. For an instant I thought I was at home, in my bed.

Then I heard Melichetti's dog barking. And some voices. They had arrived.

I tugged him. 'Filippo! Filippo, they're here! They want to kill you. Get up.'

He panted. 'I can't.'

'Yes you can. Do you want to bet?' I knelt down and with my hands pushed him forward, among the branches, regardless of the pain. Mine, his. I must get him out of that hole. The bundles of wood scratched me but I kept pushing, gritting my teeth, till we were under the mouth of the hole.

The voices were close by. And a glare flashed on the branches of the trees.

I gripped him by the arms. 'Now you've got to stand up. You've got to. And that's that.' I pulled him up, he clung to my neck. He straightened up. 'You see, stupid? You see, you have got up, haven't you? But now you've got to climb up. I'll push you from below, but you must hold onto the edge.'

He started coughing. It sounded as if stones were shooting around in his chest. When he finally stopped, he shook his head and said, 'Without you I'm not going.'

'What?'

'Without you I'm not going.'

I put my arms round him as if he was a rag doll. 'Don't be stupid. I'll be right behind you.'

Now they seemed to be there. The dog was barking above my head.

'No.'

'You're going, do you understand?' If I let go of him he would fall down. I took him in my arms and pushed him up. 'Grab the rope, come on.'

And I felt him become lighter. He had got hold of the rope! He was on top of me. He was resting his feet on my shoulders.

'Now I'm going to push you, but keep pulling yourself up with your arms, all right? Don't let up.'

I saw his small head surrounded by the pale light of the hole.

'You're there. Now pull yourself out.'

He tried. I felt him straining unsuccessfully. 'Wait. I'll help you,' I said, grasping him by the ankles. 'I'll give you a push. You jump.' I pushed at his legs and gritting my teeth I threw him out and saw him disappear swallowed up by the hole. At the same moment I felt as if a long pointed nail had been driven into my ankle bone right through to the marrow and a cutting spasm of pain ran like an electric shock through my leg up to the groin, and I collapsed.

'Michele! Michele, I've done it! Come on.'

I belched acid air. 'I'm coming. I'm just coming.'

I tried to get up but the leg no longer responded. From the ground I tried to grab the rope but I couldn't reach it.

I heard the voices coming nearer and nearer. The sound of footsteps.

'Michele, are you coming?'

'Just a moment.'

My head was spinning, but I got on my knees. I couldn't pull myself up.

I said, 'Filippo, run for it!'

He looked down. 'Come up!'

'I can't. My leg. You run for it!'

He shook his head. 'No, I'm not going.' The light behind him was brighter.

'Run for it. They're here. Run for it.'

'No.'

'You've got to go. Please. Get away!'

'No.'

I shouted and pleaded. 'Get away! Get away! If you don't they'll kill you, don't you understand?'

He started crying.

'Get away. Get away. Please, I beg of you. Get away…And don't stop. Don't ever stop. Ever…Hide!' I fell down on the ground.

'I can't do it,' he said. 'I'm scared.'

'No, you're not scared. You're not scared. There's nothing to be scared of. Hide.'

He nodded and disappeared.

From the ground I started trying to find the rope in the dark. I touched it, but lost it. I tried again, but it was too high up.

Through the hole I saw papa. In one hand he had a pistol, in the other a torch.

He had lost.

As usual.

The light blinded me. I closed my eyes.

'Papa, it's me, Miche…'

Then came the white.

I opened my eyes.

My leg hurt. It wasn't the leg that had been hurting before. The other one. The pain was a climbing plant. A piece of barbed wire twisting round my guts. Something overwhelming. Red. A dam that has burst.

Nothing can check a dam that has burst.

A roar was increasing. A metallic roar that grew and covered everything. It throbbed in my ears.

I was wet. I touched my leg. Something thick and warm was smeared all over me.

I don't want to die. I don't want to.

I opened my eyes.

I was in a whirl of straw and lights.

There was a helicopter.

And there was papa. He was holding me in his arms. He was speaking to me but I couldn't hear. His hair shone, waving in the wind.

Lights blinded me. From the darkness black creatures and dogs appeared. They were coming towards us.

The lords of the hill.

Papa, they're coming. Run for it. Run for it.

Beneath the roar my heart was marching in my stomach.

I vomited.

I opened my eyes again.

Papa was crying. He was stroking me. His hands red. A dark figure approached. Papa looked at him.

Papa, you must run for it.

In the roar papa said, 'I didn't recognise him. Help me, please, he's my son. He's wounded. I didn't…'

Now it was dark again.

And there was papa.

And there was me.

More quality fiction from Text Publishing

FEATHERSTONE
Kirsty Gunn

Featherstone: an attractive, small rural town serving
outlying estates, bank post office, school…

'Kirsty Gunn's *Featherstone* is a parable of home and
away, darkness and light, written in a prose so exact
and musical that the novel itself may be a changeling…
A town, a world, a myth that is a story about ordinary
lives unfolds in magical transition between presence
and absence. *Featherstone* sparkles like a shard of
glass and cuts as deeply.'
Jayne Ann Phillips

'I challenge anyone not to be drawn into the lives
of these people as their world slowly unravels over
the course of a weekend after which, as is often the
case, nothing will be the same. Emotional, evocative
and, dare I say, unexpectedly erotic,
Featherstone is highly recommended.'
Australian

'Kirsty Gunn has the originality of a poet. Her dangerous
shifting territory is the underworld of female desire.'
The Times

328pp, paperback, rrp$24.95, ISBN 1 877008 12 5

THE SCARECROW
Ronald Hugh Morrieson

Text Publishing is proud to reissue this Australasian coming-of-age classic, first published in 1963.

'The Tom Sawyer of Klynham, Neddy tells a story full of extravagantly funny small-town incidents—most of them centred in his own poverty-stricken, easy-going family…Morrieson's zest for life makes his whole apparatus of grotesquerie and farce the vehicle of an affirmative and oddly enough wholesome vision… One is tempted to think that had Dickens begun his career in the twentieth century and with a novel whose major theme was sex he might very well have produced a book like *The Scarecrow*.'
Meanjin

'Such an instinct for combining the bizarre and the beautiful that I am entirely disarmed.'
C. K. Stead

'Infectious warmth and gusto…one of the most unusual and original novels published in this country for many a long day…a kind of extraordinary comic fugue, with innocence answering evil, and horror answering laughter, and ugly death answering ripe youth.'
Sydney Morning Herald

240pp, paperback, rrp$23.00, ISBN 1 877008 28 1